New Day for Dragon

New Day for Dragon

LYNN HALL

illustrated by Joseph Cellini

𝒻 Follett
Publishing
Company

Chicago

ISBN 0–695–40515–2 Titan binding
ISBN 0–695–80515–0 Trade binding

Library of Congress Catalog Card Number: 74-83606

First Printing

Chapter One

The horse stood on splayed legs in the middle of the stream while the water made moving rings around his knees. His head hung low, ears relaxed. He teetered between drinking from the stream and rolling in it. Finally, grunting, he lowered himself into the six-inch depth of the water and rolled over, half in and half out of the stream. From side to side he kicked himself, legs flailing, body twisting, withers digging into the cool sand of the stream bank. He grunted again and again at the luxury of sand grating against fly bites.

Two men stood under a tree some distance away, and watched.

"Three hundred, four hundred, five hundred," the larger man said.

"Five hundred what?"

Mr. Burr looked away from the horse and grinned at his foreman. "Didn't you ever hear that old horseman's rule? A horse is worth a hundred dollars for every time it'll roll clear over on its back. Old Dragon just rolled five times in a row."

The men watched silently for a few minutes. Then the foreman said, "How much *do* you reckon he'll bring?"

Burr narrowed his eyes and gave a long sniff. "It's hard to say about an auction. Depends on the crowd. Might be a thousand; might be twice that much. All I know is they got POA breeders from all over the country coming to bid on him."

The foreman shook his head. "I still don't see why you want to sell a gold mine like Dragon. The stud fees he's brought in the last few years oughta keep you in whiskey the rest of your life."

Burr laughed. "Yeah, that old stud's done pretty good for me, all right, considering I only paid twenty-four dollars for him. But I got better studs coming up, don't forget—sons of his out of those good Arab and quarter mares, and they're a darn sight easier to handle than that old cuss down there. He ain't never going to be nothing but a wild stud at heart, and a horse like that's a dang nuisance to have around. Besides, he's fifteen years old. He's not going to bring top dollar for much longer. Best to get rid of him now while he's still worth something."

With a great and gratifying splash Dragon came to his feet. He lunged up out of the stream, flapped a spray of sand and water off of himself, and galloped across the field, bucking every few strides because it felt so good.

It was March and midmorning, and the day was already hot. A jet screamed down low over the pasture, approaching the Dallas airport, but Dragon didn't race its shadow as he sometimes did. He couldn't completely relax while the men were in the pasture.

Dragon watched the men while he grazed. They were mounted now, and driving some of his colts into the small pen in the corner of the pasture. The stock truck was backed up to the loading chute at the far side of the pen, and one by one the yearling colts disappeared into the blackness of the truck box.

A few years ago Dragon would have fought the men who took his colts away from him, just as he had once fought marauding stallions in the Mexican mountains. But now his life was settled into other patterns. Compromises had been made.

He lifted his head. The men were riding toward him. Warily he chewed the grass that protruded like whiskers from his lips. He moved away from the men at an easy trot, not yet worried about them but unwilling to let them get too close. They maneuvered his movements with the movements of their horses, no one going fast but everyone working gradually toward the holding pen. Dragon knew where they wanted him; he knew he would eventually be inside the pen, and past experience had told him nothing very bad happened to him inside that pen, yet he went through the choreography of resistance. It must not be too easy for the men.

He was inside the pen, with the gate shut behind him, before he was aware of the threat of the truck, whose giant black mouth stretched to swallow him. From inside the truck box came the sounds of yearling colts moving restlessly, bumping each other. The smell of their fear multiplied Dragon's terror of the truck. The stink of the truck itself filled his head and blinded his eyes and brought the terrifying memory back to life.

Again, headlights bored into his brain, his mares screamed and bled and died, his own body was struck and tossed to the edge of death. White highway lights and wailing sirens became a whirlpool that pulled him down through its coils.

His head cleared and came back to now, but his body was trembling and soaked with sweat.

Three years had passed since the night he had tried to take his mares south to their mountains for foaling time and had led them, instead, to slaughter on the interstate highway, but his fear of trucks was only slightly faded.

Now the men, dismounted, were inside the pen with him, and the maneuvering began again. This time it was the loading chute, and the truck behind it, toward which they pushed him. They pushed just with the presence of their bodies, moving left or right as he did, cutting off his escape. Time after time he bolted between the men, but there was nowhere to go except around the pen again.

Burr shouted. "This could take all day. We got to get on the road. Use the cattle prod."

The foreman ran in close to Dragon and pointed at his hindquarters with a shining stick. Dragon flattened his ears. The stick bit him so sharply with its electric bite that, in one motion, he kicked out and bolted forward. He was up the chute and into the truck before the terror let go of him.

"Ahhh," the foreman yelled. He grabbed his left knee and swore a savage breath full of oaths. Then, limping and muttering, he slammed shut the gate of the truck box and rammed home the lock bolt.

"Better bring that prod with us," Burr called around the corner of the truck. "He might give us some trouble at the sale barn."

"I'll give *him* some trouble if he don't look out," the foreman shouted back. "That buzzard nearly broke my leg."

For the next six hours Dragon rode with his legs braced against the swaying of the truck and his muscles knotted with fear. When at last the movement stopped and the gate was opened, he was exhausted.

He and the colts clattered down the chute but found no freedom at the other end, only an alleyway crammed with horses. He felt the jolt of concrete through his hooves; he scraped against a stout white board fence higher than his head; he craned away from a black sky that was not sky but roof. From all sides his ears were assaulted by the roar of truck motors, the laughter and shouts of close-packed people, the nervous whinnying of horses he couldn't see.

There was a small raised office at one side of the alley, where two women in denim jackets wrote on pads, took money, handed out large stickers with numbers on them. From above and behind him, someone smacked Dragon on the rump and left a white paper circle glued there, bearing the number "42." The colts were similarly marked. Then there was more shouting, a gate opened, and the tide of colts carried Dragon down a broad sawdust aisle and into another pen.

Here, as in the alleyway, Dragon was held by plank walls higher than his head. The pen was square, dimly lit, and just big enough for him and the nine yearlings to stand or to mill about uneasily. Dragon disliked the closeness of the colts. They bumped him and added their fears to his own.

He became gradually aware of the people beyond the boards, standing on the boards to look over the top, peering between the boards, banging against the boards to rattle his nerves. Many of them were small and had high quick voices unlike any Dragon had ever heard. Their differentness upset him, and yet he sensed that the danger came from the big hard-voiced people rather than from the smaller ones.

"Hey, I think this is him over here. Isn't that him?"

"Is that Dragon? Let me see. Where?"

"That big one in the middle, stupid. The other ones are all colts. Don't you know anything? Hey, Dad, this is Dragon over here."

"Boy, you'd think they would have at least brushed him up a little bit. Look at those burrs in his tail, man. And his mane."

"Lookit. He's got mud all over him."

"He's wild and woolly and full of fleas, and never been curried below the knees."

Laughter prickled at Dragon.

The crowd outside the pen grew.

"So that's the famous Dragon, huh? Got a nice head on him."

"Powerful-looking little bugger, isn't he? Doesn't show his age at all."

"How old is he, anyway, Sam?"

"Oh, they reckon about fifteen. Don't know for sure, of course, beings as he was born wild. Looks like a three-year-old, don't he? I might do a little bidding on him myself."

"You figure he'll be worth it? He's bound to go for a good price, with the reputation he's got as a producer."

"Well, of course that depends on how much a fellow would have to pay for him. But I'll tell you, I've seen quite a few colts he's sired, and he sure throws good stuff. Sound little rascals, every one of them, and just about all appaloosa-marked, and every one of them had a kind of class about him— can't quite say what it was. The way they carry themselves, I guess. If you ask me, whoever goes out of here tonight with that little horse is going to *have* something, no matter how much he has to pay for him."

From the far end of the building came a voice that sounded unnaturally loud and tinny to Dragon.

"Testing, testing. Hey, are we plugged in? Good evening, folks. I want to welcome y'all to the first annual national Pony of the Americas sale. We got a great turnout here tonight, folks, and we want to thank y'all for coming. Those of you who came a long ways, we hope you enjoy your stay in Oklahoma City, and we hope y'all find just what you're lookin' for here tonight. We got a barn full of some awful good-lookin' horseflesh, including some pretty famous names among POAs, so just limber up that bidding hand and don't choke your checkbooks to death. You don't want to die rich, so you might as well spend it here."

Laughter.

The people outside Dragon's pen gradually drifted toward the loud voice, and Dragon allowed his muscles to relax slightly. But then the pen gate opened and one of his colts was led away. After several minutes another was led away, and then another. The colts were used to being handled, and they allowed themselves to be led. But they didn't come back.

Dragon grew tense again as he became aware that his colts, and horses from adjoining pens, were gradually disappearing. They walked down the aisle with a man at their head, and they went through a door at the end of the aisle, and they didn't come back.

Dragon sensed it would happen to him, and eventually it did. The gate opened. He stood his ground in the center of the now-empty pen until the foreman's electric stick bit him on the back and sent him bolting up the aisle and through the opened door.

"Look out, you kids. Keep out of his way. He's a wild one." Burr's voice followed Dragon.

Beyond the door Dragon slid to a startled halt. He was in another pen, hardly bigger than the truck box had been but brilliantly lighted. Along one side was a high platform holding the man with the loud voice, and around the other three sides, separated from him by just a pipe rail, was a solid jam of faces rising to the ceiling, people moving and rustling and whispering and talking and laughing and yelling. Curtains of cigar smoke curled around the lights and crept into his nostrils.

He flattened his ears and whirled, but the door behind him was closed. He stood staring, trembling, while the voice cracked through his head.

". . . the one y'all came to see, folks. Here we have a little stud horse that I think I can safely say is one of the foundation sires of the POA breed. You've all seen his offspring winning in the show ring. You've seen them win in top performance horse competition, and you've seen them win in halter classes. This here is the source of all that quality—ladies and gents, the one and only Dragon! He's not a youngster, folks; we're not going to try

16

to fool you about his age. He's got some years on him. Mr. Burr reckons him to be about fifteen, give or take a year. But you can see for yourself he's still in his prime."

Dragon moved in a tight tense circle, first one direction, then the other. He arched his neck and flared his nostrils and hated.

He was not where he was supposed to be. He was supposed to be in his pasture, with his stream and his mares. He was filled with confusion and dread.

"Now, one other thing, folks. Mr. Burr says to tell you this here ain't no kids' pony. This is a stallion that's lived wild most of his life, and he ain't used to being handled, so we don't want nobody buying him with the idea he's going to be a back-yard pet. He's a working stallion, and his colts are smart and trainable and as gentle as you'd want, but *he's* not that easy, and we don't want nobody getting hurt. Okay, let's start the bidding."

Two men appeared on either side of the pen. They carried slim canes, and they faced the crowd and scanned it for a sign of a bid.

The loud voice said, "Who'll start us off at five hundred?"

Almost instantly one of the cane-bearers pointed his cane at a man in the crowd and yelped, "Hyup."

"Five-five-five, gimme six," the voice called.

18

"Hyup."

"Who'll make it a thousand?"

"Hyup."

"Thousand-thousand-thousand, gimme twelve. . . . Twelve, we have twelve. Gimme fifteen. . . . Fifteen-fifteen—sixteen! Who'll give me eighteen, eighteen? Got it! Two thousand, two-two-two."

"Hyup."

"Gimme twenty-five. This is the one and only Dragon, folks. Twenty-five hundred dollars is all we're askin'. You can't take it with you. Gimme twenty-five."

"Hyup."

"Twenty-six, twenty-six, six-six-six-six—"

"Hyup."

"Twenty-eight."

There was no response. The cane-bearers searched the faces that rose to the ceiling around them. The smoke wafted around the lights. The room grew quiet.

"Sold! Sold for twenty-six hundred dollars, to Tom Hunter from up Iowa-way. Okay, boys, move him out of here."

Chapter Two

Dragon spent the night circling his pen in the back of the sale barn. By the time the sun, and his visitors, arrived, he was weary.

Four of them stood on the boards of his pen and looked over the top at him—Mr. Burr, another man, a woman, and someone similar to a man but with an aura of youth about him, like one of Dragon's yearling colts. Until yesterday Dragon had not been close to any type of human other than the cowboys who had captured him in Mexico and the similar cowboys on the ranch in Texas who brought him mares and took his colts. As he watched these four, from the far side of his pen, he sensed little threat from the woman and the coltlike man. Even the other man, standing next to Burr, seemed less fearsome than Burr did. This man had a quieter voice, a different mixture of smells, a smoother way of moving.

The boy spoke. "I can hardly wait to show him to the kids at school." His voice had a strange crackling quality, jumping from high to low. Dragon flicked his ears.

"Now listen, Lyle," the woman said. "You remember what we told you. This one isn't going to be like the other ponies. You kids are going to have to stay away from him, hear?"

"Oh, Mom."

"Your ma's right," Burr said. "I wasn't just popping my gums when I said I wasn't selling him as no kids' pony. For all practical purposes he's as wild as the day he come out of the mountains. I wouldn't want anybody getting hurt, now."

The man said, "Has he had any training at all? Is he lead-broke even?"

Burr chewed his lip. "Well now, Mr. Hunter, I couldn't say for sure about that. He was being rode the first time I saw him, but it was purely against his will, and I think he was just plain outweighed in that little contest. He was more or less halter-broke at that time, you could say, but I haven't handled him enough to amount to a hill of beans the three years I've had him. I just drive him in the pen when he's got a mare to breed, and drive him back out again. He ain't really mean, not like a killer. I reckon he'd be safe enough to work around if you messed with him some, but at his age he ain't never going to get broke to ride, nor nothing like that."

"Hey," the boy said brightly, "I just realized— Dragon is older than I am."

No one paid attention to him.

Mrs. Hunter craned to look around her husband at Mr. Burr. "How did you happen to find Dragon anyway? I read that article about him in the POA magazine, but it didn't go into much detail."

Burr lifted his hat and scratched his head. "Oh, I'd got kind of interested in the idea of these POA ponies, you know, starting a new breed and all. Reckon I wanted to get in on the ground floor, so to speak. There was a few good studs, Black Hand and Siri Chief, but they wasn't getting a very high percentage of the appaloosa coloring in their colts. Good colts, but they just wasn't breeding as true for color as what the breeders wanted.

"Well sir, ma'am, I'd been down in Mexico a time or two, buying mustangs, and I got to thinking about all them little herds of wild ponies they had down there. They was about the size for a POA, and most all either pintos or appaloosie-colored. So I reckoned I might find a little ap stallion down there somewhere that I could pick up cheap, that would breed true for the ap coloring, since them wild horses are all so inbred they reproduce pretty true.

"Anyways, I got off on some little old back road down there, and here come that little Dragon horse down the road carrying the fattest old Mexican cowboy you ever saw—must of been a good three hundred pounds, that guy. Big heavy stock saddle that dang near covered the whole pony. Hundred-pound sack of corn tied on behind the saddle, and that old cowboy was leading a pig on a rope. Going into town to the slaughterhouse to make that little horse into dog food.

"I found out later there'd been a government bounty offered for Dragon, dead or alive. Him and his mares had been doing a lot of crop damage, they said. They'd just rounded him up the day before. I guess that cowboy just threw a saddle on him and rode him till he was wore down to a nubbin, and then headed for town with him."

"So that was all the breaking he's had," Lyle said.

"That's it, kiddo."

For a few minutes they watched Dragon and Dragon watched them. He could feel something about to happen.

Mr. Hunter pulled in a big breath and said, "Well, family, we've got a long drive ahead of us. We'd better get him loaded."

The gate swung open, and Dragon was herded, more gently this time, down the aisle, into the concrete alleyway, up a loading chute, and into the narrowest truck he had ever seen. It was barely longer than he was, and so narrow that his hips touched both sides when he tried to turn around and get out of it. He could not turn. He tried to back out but bumped his tail against the hastily slammed rear gate.

He rolled his eyes and raised his head so high his nose touched the top of his confinement. It was an arc of hard, cold, green stuff through which he could see the sky and a green-dimmed morning sun. Beneath his head was a semicircular manger filled with hay. The floor under his hooves was deeply bedded with clean straw, but through the straw he felt an unsettling unevenness in the flooring, as though hooves before his had pawed hollows in the boards.

From outside the trailer came the boy's voice. "He loaded easy enough. I don't think he's all that wild, do you, Mom?"

"You're not going to go messing with him, if that's what you're leading up to," she said. "Hop in the car, now. You want front or back?"

Their voices disappeared in the slamming of car doors, and in a few minutes Dragon's floor began to vibrate and move.

At first it frightened him to see bits of movement flashing toward his head through the curved green windshield of the trailer, and then curling past his view and out of sight. But after a few miles he understood that nothing was going to hit his face. His fear settled into uneasiness and the old sense of being off-center. This cage was pulling him north and east, just as another truck had pulled him north and east of where he and his mares belonged, seasons and seasons ago, when he had watched his mountains flashing away from him between the slats of Burr's stock truck.

Through the long morning and the longer afternoon Dragon's right front hoof made circles in the air, sometimes striking a hollow note against the manger, sometimes swishing a mound of straw back against his hind legs. When there was no more straw in the front corner of the trailer, his hoof scraped in a hopeless rhythm against the already hollowed floorboard.

Every few hours the trailer stopped. Car doors slammed, faces looked in at him through his green windows, and gasoline fumes burned the raw linings of his nostrils.

The crackling voice would say, "Hey there, Dragon. How you doing?"

The man's voice would say, "Fill 'er up, and check the oil, would you?" and the higher voice would say, "Lyle, if you want the bathroom, now's your chance. We won't be stopping again for a while," and the boy would answer, "Oh, Mom."

As afternoon became evening and evening became night, Dragon's restlessness grew. His legs were cramped from standing so long in one place, and his feeling of being too far north became more and more acute.

The trailer began to sway around curves more frequently as the night went on, and to tilt uphill, then downhill. Dragon felt a sense of mountains; not his own, but mountains nonetheless. He wanted to be out of this infuriating cage and galloping through the mountains, going south, going where his mares were, filling the long hollows of his head with night air to ease the gasoline sting.

He raised his hoof to paw at the floor. At that instant the trailer swayed and threw his weight onto the lifted leg. It came down, hard, on the hollowed wood.

Something cracked.

Suddenly Dragon was on his knees and pain was coming in waves up his right foreleg. He grunted and bared his teeth against the pain.

A stream of air rushed up into the trailer, blowing bits of straw against Dragon's face, but he didn't notice. There was something terrifyingly wrong with his leg. It was outside the trailer, hanging down

outside, bending back, blowing back, riding, bouncing against the highway below.

The pain was intense.

Slowly Dragon's hindquarters sank to the straw, and his left front leg curled under the lowered weight of his body. His neck was pushed awkwardly to the side of the hay manger, and there was no comfortable place to put his head.

He tried again and again to heave his weight up and back far enough to get his good front leg under him, but when he pulled up on the leg that hung beneath the trailer, the broken floorboard closed against the leg and held it in a splintery bite.

With each attempt to raise himself Dragon's muscles grew weaker. They ached and made small spasmodic jumping movements when he relaxed them. His body was coated with sweat that began to lather.

A new element came into the pain of hoof grating against cement. Live flesh was beginning to be touched. Dragon's breath came in small grunting puffs.

Relentlessly the car and trailer sailed through the night, moving diagonally north and east across Missouri, through the upper foothills of the Ozarks and out onto the flat Missouri farmland. Once the mountains were past, the car picked up speed.

28

Pain and terror had equal holds on Dragon's mind, and they were augmented by flashes of memory—truck headlights and white highway lights and roaring motors and squealing mares and the whacking overwhelming pain of truck fender against his side. His hatred for trucks grew deeper and more intense with every wave of fire that burned up the nerves of his leg. The wall of air struck raw muscles now, and bare bone, and it was no longer dead hoof but live, screaming quick that bumped and grated on the pavement.

He closed his eyes against the blowing chaff that irritated them, and let his head sink crookedly to the floor. There was nothing to do but endure.

Gradually he became aware that the trailer was no longer moving. He opened his eyes. Outside a car door slammed, then another and another. Bright lights shone in through the green windshield, and the smell of gasoline was sharp.

Dragon made a rattling attempt at rising, but failed.

The boy's face appeared at the window.

"Dragon! Hey! Dad! Come here quick. Dragon's down. Something's wrong with him."

Other faces, other voices, floated around Dragon's head. The tailgate rattled and opened, but no one entered.

From somewhere low the boy's voice said, "My

gosh, Dad, his leg's gone through the floor. Oh, look at it. Oh, my gosh."

The trailer rocked with activity as Mr. Hunter, then the gas station attendant, then everyone, stepped on and off the trailer, kneeled beside it to peer at the trapped leg, reached under to grasp the broken floorboard in attempts to wrench it off.

From a little distance came the woman's voice. "Oh, my God, he's broken his leg. We didn't even get him home and he's broken his leg already and we're going to have to shoot him."

Mr. Hunter spoke breathlessly from a doubled-over position at the side of the trailer. "I don't think the leg is broken, Ruth, though heaven only knows why it isn't. Get down here and take a look at it. See? It looks straight enough; it's just scraped something fierce. Look at that hoof. It's worn half away. It must have been dragging a long time. I didn't hear a thing, did you? Poor old Dragon!"

The station attendant said, "Let me get a crowbar. We're going to have to get that piece of board off of there before you can do anything else."

Dragon lay listening. The throbbing in his leg was growing more intense now, without the numbing effect of the rushing air. His good front leg ached almost unbearably, too, from being curled so long under the weight of his body.

The people outside began jostling and banging

against the board that was cutting into his leg. He groaned softly as their movements sent fresh pain up into his head. Weakly, miserably, he hated them all.

Suddenly, with a ripping sound, the chunk of board fell away. Now the hole in the floor was well over a foot long, and nothing was holding his leg. He tried to pull the aching thing up under him, but he was too weak, too off-balance.

The people came around to the tailgate. "I need to get in there," Mr. Hunter mused. "If I could get up by his head and grab hold of his halter, I might be able to help him brace enough to stand up. We've got to get him up on his feet."

Dragon watched them through eyes tearing against the straw chaff. When the man moved toward his hindquarters, as the foreman used to do with his biting stick, Dragon flattened his ears and cocked a hind hoof into kicking position. He could tolerate no more fear nor pain.

"You're not going to go climbing around his legs, Tom," the woman said. "He'll kick the stuffings out of you."

There was a noise and a puff of air from above Dragon's head. The boy said, "Hey, Dad, I could crawl in here, through the hay door, and get hold of his head. He couldn't kick me from there."

Faces and voices shifted to the front of the trailer. Mr. Hunter's head and one of his shoulders came through the small door above the hay manger.

"Shoot! The dratted door's too small for me to get through."

"I can get through, Dad. I have before. Let me."

The woman said, "I don't want you in there with that horse, Lyle. That's too dangerous."

The voices went on. Dragon breathed and grunted small grunts and made another weak attempt at getting to his feet. Suddenly the boy was coming at him, head first, slowly, slowly creeping through the small door into the hay manger.

"Easy, Dragon; easy now; easy, boy," the voice chanted softly. "I'm going to help you. Don't be scared."

Dragon rolled his eyes and tried to twist his head so he could watch the boy.

Mr. Hunter called softly, "Get that lead rope that's down under the hay, there. Can you find it?"

"Yeah. Got it."

"Okay. See if you can get it snapped onto his halter, but be awful careful. Don't let him bite you."

A wad of rope in the boy's fist came slowly, carefully, toward Dragon's muzzle. He stared at it.

"Easy now; easy, boy."

The rope stopped where Dragon could smell it. He smelled a sweat of fear on the boy's hand, and the smell made his heart pound.

32

The boy's fingers moved and opened the snap at the end of the rope. Dragon tensed. He flicked his ears forward and back. A new sweat broke over his neck.

The hand and the rope moved down toward the halter ring under his chin. For an instant the boy's bare wrist lay against Dragon's nostril, blocking his air. His lips stretched and tightened.

He felt a fumbling touch against his halter, a small pull, a snap. He flattened his ears. Then the hand was withdrawn.

"Okay, Dad. I got the rope on his halter. He didn't even try to bite me. What should I do now?"

"See if you can just, I don't know, pull up on his head, give him whatever leverage you can while I try to push the leg up from underneath. You be careful, though. Stay out of his road all you can, and don't get out of the manger, you hear?"

"Okay."

Something touched the dangling leg, and the pain sent Dragon scrambling up and back, away from it. This time nothing held the leg down. He flailed and kicked and would have rocked back down except for a sudden pressure against his head. He was sitting, and then, with a huge heave, he was standing. He wove dizzily, but he stood, the injured leg curled up away from the floor.

"He's up! He's up!" The boy's voice was jubilant but softened. Outside there were sighs and chattering relieved voices.

Mr. Hunter looked in the hay door. "Why don't you tie the rope to the manger and crawl on out? I think he'll ride okay now."

"Are we going to try to find a vet?"

"Well, I think our best bet would be just to get him on home. It's not much farther now, and I don't much want to try to find a strange vet in a strange town at two in the morning, besides the fact that the nearest town is fifteen miles. And I don't want to have to load and unload him any more than necessary. I think we'd best just get him on home."

"Well, let me ride back here with him then, Dad. What if his leg goes through the hole again? We wouldn't hear him. We didn't, before. I know what. Why don't you give me the flashlight, and if I need help, I can shine it at you through the window. Okay?"

"You're sure he's not going to hurt you in there?"

"I don't think so, and you know I'm no hero around horses. He looks like he doesn't feel good enough to do any more than just stay on his feet."

"Well, okay. We'll be home in an hour or so anyway. You stay in there, and be careful. Ruth, get the flashlight out of the glove compartment, will you?"

The journey began again, and the motion of the trailer renewed the hurt in Dragon's leg. The boy was in front of him, too close, too close to his head. He wanted to move away, but could not. Small waves of the fear smell came from the boy every now and then. The boy's voice went on and on and became part of the pain and the fear and the old and new hates that lay heavily inside the little stallion.

Chapter Three

The trailer slowed, slowed, stopped, moved backward, and stopped again. The boy, who had been
dozing in the manger, woke and stretched his neck.
Dragon tensed.

"We're home, old buddy."

Small clankings and jigglings came from behind Dragon. When he turned his head to watch, he
found that the soreness from his leg had spread up
the side of his neck. The back end of the trailer
disappeared, letting in the night. With much cramp-
ing and banging into side walls, Dragon managed to
turn around. Just a few feet away, at the bottom
of the trailer ramp, a barn door slid back and a light
came on.

Dragon stretched out his head warily. The man

and the woman stood on either side of the ramp, cutting off his escape. He wanted to be out of the trailer, but he feared the barn and its bright yellow light. Suddenly something slapped him on the rump. He bolted down the ramp and into the barn, carrying his injured leg high. The barn was a dead end. There was nowhere to go except through one small open door. He hobbled through, and the door slammed shut behind him.

The smell of horses was heavy here. Dragon paced in a small circle, touching the four too-close walls with his nose as he went. Underfoot was a slippery softness, something like hay. In one wall was a high dusty window that showed a streak of gray in the sky.

The door opened a bit, and a bucket of water appeared on the floor. He wanted to drink, but feared the vulnerability of lowering his head into the bucket.

"Okay, Son," the man said. "He'll be all right for now. Let's get in the house and try to get a little sleep. It's been a long day."

Dragon saw a slice of the boy's face between the boards of the door. " 'Night, Dragon," the voice whispered.

When the people had gone, some of the tension eased out of Dragon's muscles. He needed to be out of this stall, this barn, this foreign place where he could smell no trace of his mares or his pasture, but at least he was free from the immediate threat of the people, and especially the boy, who was connected in some way with the pain in his leg. He moved through the rustling softness that followed his hooves, and took a long pulling drink from the water bucket. The water didn't taste right. He moved away and touched his nose to the hay that spiked out from a corner hayrack, but he didn't eat. The small strange noises around him worried him. Above his head something rustled. He heard a meow from up there, and tiny cries. A dog barked in the distance and set two others to barking near the barn. Every now and then he heard a strange rushing, pinging sound growing closer and then fading into the distance.

He rustled over to the small high window and rested the cushion of his chin on its sill.

It was much later in the morning when the barn door squeaked open and four figures approached Dragon's stall. They were smaller than the people Dragon was used to seeing. He heard the boy's crackling voice among the higher-pitched voices of the others, and he tensed and turned away from the window so that they couldn't sneak up on him.

Four sets of toes poked through the slats of his door, and four heads popped up above it.

"So that's the famous Dragon, huh? He sure looks cruddy and dirty."

"Hi, Dragon. Here, boy; here, boy."

"Hey, Lyle, he's neat. I bet he'll be fun to ride."

"Well, you'll never know, Rocky. You heard what Dad said. We're not supposed to mess around with him."

"Yeah, but you're not really going to not mess around with him, are you? I bet *I* could ride him. He doesn't look so mean to me, and if I can handle Midnight, I can handle anything."

"Oh, you think you're so smart."

"Well . . ."

"It's a deep subject."

"Ho, ho. You think you're so smart, just because you got to go down to the sale with Mom and Dad, but that doesn't give you first dibbies on Dragon. I can ride circles around you, and you know it. What do you want to bet I'm riding him before you are?"

Lyle's voice cracked upward. "Rocky, I'm not going to bet with you. That is a wild stallion in there, in case you forgot, and no twelve-year-old girl is going to ride him, and if I bet with you, you'll try it and get your silly self killed."

"I suppose you think a fourteen-year-old boy could do better," she taunted.

"I know darn well I couldn't. I'm not arguing the fact that you're a better rider than I am. All I'm saying is I've got better sense than to try it with him."

The smallest voice said, "Hey, here comes Doc Buck."

Mrs. Hunter and a strange man came into Dragon's view. The woman said, "You kids hop down from there now, and stay out of Doc's way. Here he is, Doc, but watch out for him. He's pretty wild."

The stall door opened, and the man came inside. He carried something black and bulky. Dragon's ears moved nervously back and forth as he tried to watch the man, the faces over the door, and the black thing on the floor. He flattened his ears and turned his head away, but the man caught the rope that still dangled from his halter, and snubbed his head up tight to the hayrack. Dragon could move his hind-quarters but not his front end. He swung his rear toward the man, but the man was already standing close to his head, safely out of kicking range. There was nothing to do but flatten his ears more tightly and try to keep the man in range of his right eye.

"My God, Ruth, he's worn away half his hoof, and that leg is scraped down to the bare bone.

40

Went through the floor of the trailer, you say?"

"Yes, and who knows how far that poor leg got dragged along the highway. We just happened to see it when we stopped for gas. It's not broken, is it?"

"No, but I don't know why it isn't. On any other horse that leg would be hanging there in pieces. This old boy must have cannon bones of solid steel. I've never seen anything like it in my life."

The man's hand touched the pillar of fire that was Dragon's leg. Dragon bared his teeth and snapped, but the halter stopped his head short of its goal.

"Easy there. I'm trying to help," the man said.

"Are you going to be able to do anything for him?" Lyle asked.

"Oh, we'll give 'er a try. That hoof is pretty far gone, but there's not much we can do about that except try to keep a pack on it, to keep the air and bedding off those raw nerves, and hope the hoof will grow back. Same with the rest of the leg. I can't take stitches; it's too wide a wound. It'll just have to fill in from the inside out."

"Is he going to be okay?" one of the other small voices asked.

"I don't know, Jimmy. I've never seen anything like this before. What I'll do, I'll give him a shot of a pretty hefty tranquilizer now, and load him up with antibiotics, and then I'll stop back in a couple of hours, when he's doped up, and put a pack on it. Nobody's going to handle that leg now, as sore as it must be. I'll call the veterinary college at the university, at Ames, when I get back to the office, and see if they know anything more to do for him."

While he talked, the man opened his bag and filled two syringes. Dragon felt a prick of pain in his flank, and then another, like the bites of the vampire bats that tormented him when he was a colt.

"Best leave him tied where he is," the man said as he left the stall. "I'll be back after lunch."

Everyone left except Lyle, who slipped into the stall and sat down on the straw in the corner, where Dragon could see him. The boy seemed less threatening when he became so low to the ground.

"I'll stay here and keep you company."

The boy sat so quietly that after a while Dragon forgot to watch him. Dragon's ears began buzzing in a curiously unfrightening way, and his vision blurred. He thought about lying down in the long grass by a mountain stream, close to where his dam was grazing. He teetered a bit and moved to set down his right foreleg so that he could relax a hip, but when the foreleg brushed close to the straw, the pain made him start. His eyes blinked; his heart pounded. He found that when he wanted to move his head, it moved in a slow, jerky way and not quite in the direction he intended. This seemed curious.

He became aware that the man with the strange black object was standing at his side, bending over his injured foreleg, doing something to it. Dragon moved to withdraw the leg from the man's hands, but the leg seemed to want to stay where it was. There was a coolness against his hoof and a tightness high on his leg that seemed to hold the pain in check.

After a while the man wasn't there any more, but someone was standing close to Dragon's side. A voice faded in and out of Dragon's mind, and it seemed to him that something was scratching lightly down the length of his neck. It might have been the rough tongue of the mare who dried him off after his birth-journey, or it might have been grass or the bark of a tree or the sandy bank of the creek that crossed his pasture. He leaned into it and shivered his skin with pleasure.

It moved down his neck and his body, down his left hind leg as far as his knee, but then it felt more like flies bothering him than tree bark and he wanted to kick at it, but there was something wrong with his front end that made it impossible to raise his hind hoof. The scratching stopped, though, and became a series of gentle pulls at his tail. He shook his head to try to clear his thinking so he would know if there was a danger in the pulling at his tail.

He realized suddenly that small clumping noises were coming at him from directly above his head, and a dusting of hay chaff was sifting down on him. When the bits of dust and hay floated through the sunlight from the window, they became live and eerie and frighteningly close to his face. He threw his head back sharply.

Very near his ear a voice said loudly, "Hey, you kids, quit making so much noise in the loft. You're scaring Dragon."

"We're not making any noise. We were just looking at the kittens." _

"Well, cut it out, will you? I'm brushing Dragon, and you're scaring him."

There were more rustling noises, then small scrapes as cowboy boots descended the loft ladder.

"Hey, you really are brushing him," Jimmy said as he hung over the stall door.

"He's going to kick the daylights out of you," Rocky added.

"No, he's not. Old Dragon knows a friend when he meets one. Lookit. I got this whole side of him brushed, and his mane mostly combed out, and I made a dent in all those mats in his tail—at least, till you kids spooked him."

"Oh, Lyle." Rocky's voice was heavy with disdain. "He's all doped up from that shot Doc Buck gave him. That's the only reason he hasn't kicked the daylights out of you. Why don't you get on him? I dare you."

Dragon's head was growing clearer. His vision and hearing were almost normal now, and only his reflexes were still slowed. The boy was standing close to his side, where Dragon could reach him with neither teeth nor hooves, and rubbing at his skin with something scratchy. Dragon flattened his ears and bared his teeth and was rewarded by the smell of the boy's fear.

Lyle stepped cautiously away. "I'm not going to get on him. He's got a hurt leg, for Pete's sake."

"And besides, you're scared of him," Rocky added.

From beyond the barn a voice called, "Kids. Come get washed up for supper."

Rocky and Jim disappeared, but Lyle paused at the stall door. "I'm sorry you didn't like the brushing, Dragon. Did it hurt you or scare you? Or are you just too dignified to be handled like that? Is it hard for you to be a kids' pet after all those years of being king of the mountains? Hmm, I wonder if horses do have feelings like that."

Quiet evening came into the barn, and Dragon sagged into near-sleep. He was not in the right place; he was surrounded by dangers he could not even recognize, but his muscles and his brain could stay alert no longer.

Chapter Four

As the days went by, the soreness in Dragon's leg began to drain away. For the first few weeks the man with the black bag came every two or three days, and during the sleep times that accompanied the man's visits, he unwrapped and rewrapped the leg and patted Dragon's shoulder.

At first Dragon spent most of his time tied in the corner of the stall, but after Mr. Hunter pronounced him sufficiently settled down, he was allowed the freedom of the stall. Later he was released into the long broad alley of the barn twice a day to trot and shake his head and ease the kinks from his muscles. It was always the boy who opened the stall door.

The days developed a schedule, and although it was irksome in its confinement, the schedule brought some element of reassurance to Dragon. Early each morning the boy turned him out into the aisle, patting his neck as he surged through the stall door. When those welcome minutes of movement were over and the boy herded him back into the stall, he found fresh bedding, new water in the bucket, and a renewed supply of hay in the corner rack. Late in the afternoon the exercise period was repeated, but then the boy followed him back into his stall, tied him to the hayrack, and brushed him.

At first Dragon resented the brushing. He bared his teeth at the boy, knowing and resenting the superiority of the boy's position. Dragon's head was tied. He could not bite, and the boy knew it. Several days passed before Dragon realized, through his anger, that nothing the boy did actually harmed him.

This realization confused the little stallion. First there had been the men who rode into his mountains when his mares were heavy with foal and could not escape them. Those men had roped him, dragged him bodily out of his mountains and into a world of fences and hay. The worst of the men had hurt and humiliated him with something that wrapped itself around his head and tore at his mouth, with heavy, shifting, pinching weight on his back, and with pulling him off his feet, kicking his ribs raw with their spiked legs, and shouting into his sensitive ears.

Then there were the men at the other place,

men who struck him with electric prods and crashed into him with their trucks.

Now there were these small, high-voiced people with the sense of coltish youth. about them. They touched him, but nothing painful happened. This boy who brushed him was connected in some way with the pain in his leg, but also with the hay and water and moments of freedom in the barn aisle. Although Dragon didn't like the boy's hands to come near his head, he found that when the boy lifted the part of his halter that went behind his ears, and brushed under there, it felt surprisingly good, and he leaned into the bristles of the brush.

One day during the brushing Lyle leaned across Dragon's back. Dragon threw his head up and craned to see what the boy was doing. That pressure on his back had something to do with the man who had hurt his mouth years ago.

"It's okay, old buddy," said Lyle soothingly. "I'm not going to get on you. I'm just leaning here. See? That doesn't hurt you, does it?"

Dragon stood still, waiting.

"I wish you'd let me ride you, though. I'll tell you, it's not easy living in this family and not being the world's greatest rider. Rocky never lets me forget that she's only twelve years old and she broke Midnight all by herself. She's got ribbons and trophies up the gazoo, Dragon. All over her room.

Boy, just once I'd like to, well, I don't know what. Something. There, see? You let me lean on your back for a whole minute and the world didn't come to an end, did it? I bet I could ride you, if I took it slow enough and just worked into it."

Dragon turned his head as far as the rope would allow. The boy's voice was beginning to be a pleasant thing in his ears. But when Lyle leaned again on his back, Dragon moved away, and the boy's weight disappeared.

A few days later Mr. Hunter came to the barn with Lyle. They walked past Dragon's stall to the far end of the barn. Dragon heard the heavy barn doors rolling open, saw a broad bar of sunlight shining in, smelled the wet springtime—and mares. He laid his head on the top of the stall door and whinnied.

Lyle came. "Hey, old buddy, Doc Buck says you can go out in the barn lot for a while today, soak up some of that sunshine. I bet that'll feel good, won't it?"

Lyle's hand reached to touch Dragon as the boy opened the stall door, but Dragon's entire self was focused on that patch of gold at the end of the barn. He arched his neck and cantered down the aisle and out into the beautiful watery April sunlight. He shook his head from side to side and felt his mane slapping around his ears. It was disappointing to find only a small circle of churned and crusted mud surrounded by a high board fence, when what he wanted was a long grassy meadow to thunder through, but the freedom from the barn was enough for now. He galloped around and around the barn lot, bucking and grunting every few steps and shaking his head till his halter rings knocked against the fine bones of his face.

Standing in the barn doorway, Mr. Hunter said to Lyle, "How would you like to be up on him now?"

Lyle said nothing, and his father looked at him curiously.

Dragon stopped circling and stood with his neck stretched to full length, his muzzle over the top of the high fence. On the other side were mares. He couldn't see them except as small dark blurs in the distance, but his stallion's senses flooded his body with excitement. Mares, and some of them were ready for breeding. Of all the instincts contained in that small vital animal, the strongest were the instincts of survival, not just survival of the individual, but of the herd; and survival meant breeding every mare. He did not understand that there was a connection between the act of breeding and the foal that arrived eleven months later. He only knew he must find a way to follow the urges that were so strong within him.

"I'm sure glad Doc gave us the go-ahead to start using him for breeding," Lyle said, "with those mares coming in season early. It would have been awful if we'd had to miss a whole year because of his leg."

"You can say that again. I've got quite an investment tied up in that pony. But he doesn't seem to be favoring that leg at all today, does he?"

"Doesn't seem to. When are you going to breed the mares, Dad?"

"We'll try tomorrow with the Welsh bay mare, and probably the next day or the day after with the Arab. It's a little early yet for the other three, I think. We'll bring the bay up in the lot after we get home from church. Well, listen, I think he's had enough exercise for his first time out, and we better get ready for supper if we're going to the ball game."

"Okay. Wait a minute. Let me see if I can catch him."

Dragon was so intent upon the distant mares that he didn't see the boy until Lyle's hand reached for his halter. He snaked his head aside, beyond the boy's grasp, but moved only a step or two away. The boy reached again, and Dragon circled away from him, annoyed at the interruption in his gazing.

"Watch out he doesn't kick you," Mr. Hunter called.

"He's never tried to kick me."

51

"Well, just don't take chances."

Lyle came close again and, moving slowly, got his fingers around the halter. Dragon snatched his head aside and broke the boy's grip. But he knew he was going back into the barn. He trotted back and forth across the lot while the man and the boy walked and waved their arms and gradually pressed him into the barn aisle, then into his stall.

"Well, that wasn't as bad a job as I thought it might be," Mr. Hunter said. "Let's leave the barn door open, let a little fresh air in."

"He's really not all that wild, Dad, you know? Except for the fact that he hasn't been handled. I'm beginning to feel he's kind of a neat old horse."

The two disappeared, and Dragon was left straining to see the mares over the top of his stall door.

About sunset there were voices from the house, the slamming of car doors, and the roaring, pinging sound of the car throwing gravel on itself as it rolled down the lane and onto the road toward town. The place took on the silence that came when the house was empty, and the silence increased Dragon's restlessness. Around and around the stall he circled. His injured foreleg ached a bit from the afternoon's galloping, but he was barely aware of it. He stopped circling and kicked with frustration at the stall door. He kicked again. The resistance that hit his hooves was sturdy, but it had an element of giving in it. Harder and faster he kicked, shifting occasionally from one hind leg to the other.

Something splintered and broke away. He whirled and nosed at the raw place, but it was only one board in the stall door, broken and bent outward. He turned and resumed his pounding.

Another board gave way and sailed across the aisle, barely missing the offended barn cat and her train of kittens. The hole was about knee-level to Dragon, and not much wider than his head. He went on kicking. The mares were out there, and they must be bred.

He kicked away three more boards. Little was left of the door now except the sturdy square outline of it, and the wire mesh top half. The jagged hole was big enough for Dragon to get through, but it was low, too low for him to walk under. He thrust his head and neck through the opening, but was stopped by his withers.

Slowly, awkwardly, he bent his knees until his back was low enough to clear the top edge, but it was almost impossible to move his forelegs through the opening while they supported his precarious balance. It took several attempts before he got one leg through the hole, then most of his neck, and then the other foreleg. Finally, it was just a matter of arching his back downward and lowering his hind-

quarters and coming through the hole with a clumsy hopping motion. The jagged top of the hole caught and kept a scraping of hide from his back, and he banged his pasterns painfully on the way through.

But he was out!

Through the barn he galloped, while the cat stared and the kittens scattered. He sailed across the barn lot and, with a mighty effort, over the high board fence. The top board came down with him on the other side. He felt a deep pain in his injured foreleg as he landed, but he galloped on.

Toward the mares he raced, across a pasture blue with twilight shadows. Joy rang in his trumpeting voice. His legs no longer ached with barn-confinement. They extended themselves across the long lush grass, over the stream, up the tree-studded hill, and on to the high meadow where the mares waited. The wind blew from his mind the comforts of stall and hayrack, the sound of the boy's voice, and the feel of the brush on his skin. His element was this, the open land, the mares.

The sun was well up the next morning, when the sounds of shouting voices came floating up to the high end of the pasture, where Dragon and the five mares grazed. Six heads lifted from the grass; five horses began walking toward the voices. Dragon stood his ground, watching his mares walk away from him. He neighed at them, but they kept walking.

The mares were lovely creatures—two bright red bays, two sorrels, and one black with high white boots. One was a Shetland, one a Welsh, and one an Arabian; the other two were quarter-Welsh crosses.

Up over the rim of the meadow came heads— Mr. Hunter; Lyle; Mrs. Hunter; the younger children, Rocky and Jim; and even the older daughter, Ann, whom Dragon had seldom seen.

"Here he is," Lyle shouted. His voice rang with relief. "Boy, Dragon, you scared the daylights out of us."

"You didn't do the stall door much good, either," Mr. Hunter added wryly. "Well, at least he's okay. Doesn't look as though he hurt himself."

The mares clustered around the family, looking for oats. Dragon studied them uneasily, wishing they would stay at a safe distance from the people. It confused and troubled him that his mares seemed unconscious of the danger the people represented. With alarm he saw the black mare standing quietly while Rocky jumped up and down at her side and finally managed to fling her body across the horse's back, get a leg over, and wriggle to a sitting position. The mare neither bucked nor ran nor made any other move to rid herself of the girl on her back. Dragon stared.

56

"What're we going to do with him?" Lyle asked.

Mr. Hunter snorted. "It looks as if we're going to leave him in the pasture. I don't suppose he'll try to get out, since this is where the mares are. Now, for what we're going to do with *you*—you are going to get out your little saw and your little hammer and nails and build a new stall door."

"Why me? That's not fair."

The family turned and started down the hill, the black mare ambling along with them, still carrying Rocky.

"Why not you?" Mr. Hunter countered. "You seem to have adopted Dragon for your own, so you might as well take some responsibility for him."

The boy turned back. "Thanks a lot, old buddy," he called.

When the people were gone, Dragon circled his remaining mares and tried to drive them into a safe close knot. But they didn't seem to know about being herded, nor about the safety of closeness, nor indeed about any need for the safety of closeness. They evaded him good-naturedly and resumed their grazing. Eventually Dragon gave up the frustrating job and, like the mares, lowered his head to the grass.

Chapter Five

By a process so gradual Dragon was hardly aware of it, he found that he was allowing the boy to touch him, even in the freedom of the pasture, where escape was possible.

It began with the daily late-afternoon visits of Lyle and Rocky. They came inside the pasture gate and stood calling and whistling, while the girl shook a pail that made a swishing sound. At the first whistle all five of Dragon's new mares raised their heads and began grazing and walking toward the gate, with the black mare leading. For several days Dragon tried to drive them away from the danger; for the next several days he stood and watched angrily while they walked away from him and sank their muzzles, one at a time, into the bucket.

Gradually Dragon began following. He stayed well back from Lyle and Rocky, and glared when the girl took the black mare out of the pasture, as she usually did, and rode away on her toward the barn. The boy always stayed, always held the swishing bucket out to Dragon, tried to approach the stallion, talked in his soft, steady voice. The voice was not unpleasant to Dragon any more.

As spring warmed toward summer, and the daily visits became routine to Dragon, he allowed himself a small, growing curiosity about the bucket. One day, after the black mare had gone with Rocky and the other mares had drifted away, the boy dumped a small pile of the bucket's contents onto the ground. Then he retreated to the fence and stood quietly.

Dragon stared at the small heap of pale golden grain. It had an interesting smell.

He put his head down and began to graze, but the grazing moved him, by very gradual steps, toward the pile. When it was close to his muzzle, he stretched his neck without moving his feet, until his lips brushed the slithery grains. He tensed, ready to bolt. The grains gave off a strong smell of people, but a stronger smell of food.

He moved his head away, stared down at the pile with his near eye, then extended his lips until they scooped up a taste of the stuff. Quickly he

59

backed away to a safe distance to do his chewing. It *was* food, more delicious than any he had ever known, better than the corn from the mountain valleys in Mexico.

He ate the entire pile and worked his lips over the dirt until the last grain was gone.

"Want some more, Dragon? That was pretty good stuff, wasn't it?"

Dragon rolled a wary eye toward Lyle. The boy was holding out the bucket, but the risk was too great. He waited until the boy put another pile on the ground. This pile was too close to the boy for comfort, but Dragon decided to take the chance. With the greatest of caution he moved in and ate the second pile of grain, his near eye fastened on the boy.

"Good Dragon," Lyle crooned. "Those are oats, and if you play your cards right, you can have some every day. But you have to come up to me to get them."

The third pile was offered on the flat palm of Lyle's hand. Dragon accepted it. The smell of the boy's sweat was strong in Dragon's nostrils, but the grain was so good it was worth the contact with the boy.

From that point it was just a short step for Dragon to stand more or less fearlessly beside the boy each afternoon while he ate the delicious stuff, knowing the boy's hand was on his neck or his halter or his shoulder, but not minding sufficiently to move away.

When the days grew hot and the pasture grass grew knee-high, the pattern of the visits changed. Rocky and Lyle came at midmorning, and on most days the black mare left with Rocky and was gone all day. Lyle began snapping a lead rope onto Dragon's halter and tying him to a stout fence post. At first Dragon flung himself back in fear and anger, but then the oats would appear, and the food and the calmness of the boy's voice joined to steady him.

Gradually Lyle left Dragon tied for longer and longer periods, while he brushed and curried and talked.

"I'm going to ride you one of these days, Dragon, and you won't mind at all. I only weigh a hundred and twenty-eight pounds. That won't be anything for you to carry. And I promise I'll never hurt your mouth or use spurs or do anything you wouldn't like, okay? And then, when you get used to being ridden and know the rules, I'm going to start schooling you for Western performance competition. Won't that be something? Can't you just see it, Dragon? 'Ladies and gentlemen, the next barrel racer will be Lyle Hunter, of Fairfield, Iowa, on the world-famous Dragon!' Boy, would that ever shut Rocky up."

The spot along the pasture fence where the

daily tying-and-talking sessions occurred was under a trio of giant elm trees, where it was always shady and cool. It was as good a place to stand as any in the pasture, and since Dragon had no duties or interests in other parts of his territory, he began to find some mild enjoyment in the sound and the touch of the boy, aside from the oats he always brought.

One day during the brushing time Dragon became aware that Lyle had been leaning heavily across his back for some minutes. The boy's voice had droned so steadily, and the afternoon was so warm, that Dragon had been in a half-doze. He turned his head around as far as the rope allowed, and looked at the boy draped across his back. Dragon snorted and moved aside, and the boy slipped down to a more reassuring position, standing beside Dragon's shoulder.

But after a few moments Lyle began easing himself across Dragon's back again. Dragon tensed. The old terror filled his head.

The cowboy was a shifting, flapping, yelling weight on his back; flashes of movement seen in the backs of his eyes; a giant snake that was wrapped around his ribs, squeezing out his breath; and another snake clinging to his face. His mouth was split with pain.

This boy, like that remembered man, was on his back. Dragon trembled, waiting for the pain.

62

But no pain came—only the steadiness of the boy's voice and slow gentle movements, a hand pressed on his withers, a knee easing across his rump, a slow, slow shifting and settling of weight onto the hollow of his back. The boy's legs hung down on either side of Dragon's ribs.

Dragon's heart pounded. He threw his head up to the limits of the rope and locked his legs into ready position. A light sweat rose on his neck. His nostrils stretched, and his eyes widened.

And then, with a more sudden shifting, the weight was gone and Lyle was back where he belonged, standing on the ground beside Dragon's head, offering more oats, rubbing Dragon's itchy spot behind his ears, and talking on and on in a soft but bubbling happy voice.

When Lyle unsnapped the lead rope, he held onto Dragon's halter and walked a few steps with the horse before releasing him entirely.

"There now, old buddy," the boy called softly to the retreating Dragon. "I rode you and I led you. A little bit anyhow."

The next day when Lyle eased himself onto Dragon, the little horse tossed his head and rolled his eyes and moved restlessly in the semicircle the rope allowed, but when the boy continued to sit there talking and rubbing Dragon's neck, the threat seemed to lessen. Dragon ceased his dancing and stood for several minutes, puzzling at the harmlessness of holding the boy on his back.

After a few more days of this routine Dragon did not bother to dance or roll his eyes.

One day while Dragon was dozing and Lyle was sitting on him and playing with his mane, Rocky rode up to the fence on Midnight.

"Hey! You're riding him," she called.

"Quiet. You'll spook him. And don't ride up too close, will you? If he gets to moving around very much, he'll lose me, and I don't want him to find out how easy I am to dump."

Rocky reined in the black mare a little distance from the fence and sat leaning one elbow on her saddle horn and grinning. She was square-faced and, in her own words, built like a fence post. "Looks like you're doing all right," she said. "Didn't think you had the guts, frankly. How long have you been riding him?"

"About a week, if you can call it riding. And listen, don't mention it in front of Mom and Dad for a while yet, will you? I want to sort of work up to it gradually."

"In other words you don't want to tell them till you have to, right?"

Lyle sighed. "I'll have to one of these days, I know. See, I decided I want to train Dragon for barrel racing and pole bending and all that stuff, so I can—don't laugh now—so I can ride him in the International POA Show next year."

Rocky guffawed. "Boy, nothing like aiming high, is there? How's about letting me take him for a ride?"

"I don't think you better, Rock. He's just now getting so he's not scared of having me sit on him, and he knows me a lot better than you."

Rocky pushed against the cantle of her saddle and slid backward until she was seated behind the saddle, with both her elbows resting beside the horn. Midnight stood dozing, with one hind leg cocked. "I tell you what. I'll lead him while you ride him, and we can start teaching him stop and go signals."

"No, I don't think he's ready for that yet. I've just barely started teaching him to lead." Lyle slid off Dragon's back and stood with his arm across the horse's neck.

Rocky squinted down at him. "Well, if you want to go through life tied to a fence, that's okay with me. I'm going to go work Middy on the barrels." She humped herself back into the saddle, pulled Midnight around in a showy swirl, and galloped up the sloping lane toward the small flat field, near the road, where a triangle of racing barrels and a line of slim pole-bending poles waited.

Lyle sighed. "She's right, Dragon. I've got to get you so you'll lead, before I can start breaking you to the hackamore."

He untied the lead rope and began to walk along the fence. At the pull against his head Dragon braced his legs hard. He had planned to go the other direction, and the boy was interfering.

"Come on, Dragon. Just walk along with me."

Dragon twisted his powerful neck, jerking the boy off his feet. Deliberately he began to walk in his chosen direction, greatly hampered by the weight of the boy's dragging body hanging from his head.

"Whoa, Dragon. Easy now."

There was suddenly something sinister in the rustling dragging person so near his front hooves. Dragon half-reared, and his head came free. He turned and galloped away with the lead rope slapping against his chest.

Nearly two weeks passed before the leading lessons resolved into a stalemate. Dragon allowed the boy to walk beside his head so long as Lyle did not interfere with the direction or the speed. As soon as Dragon became restless at the slowness of the walking, Lyle unsnapped the rope and let him go. In the meantime the sitting sessions continued.

One afternoon Dragon realized that he was

following the boy, rather than the boy following him. He tossed his head and pulled Lyle off to the side of the path.

"Oh, heck. You were doing so well there for a while, Dragon. Oh, well, that's enough for today anyway. I won't be here tomorrow. I have to go to the dentist. You don't know how lucky you are to be a horse."

Dragon felt the lead rope unsnapping from his halter, but he lingered for a moment, until the boy's voice was finished. Then he turned and trotted away, shaking his head from side to side to assert his superiority.

The next morning Rocky came alone to the pasture, carrying the oat bucket and Midnight's bridle. But she didn't catch the black mare. Instead she let the five mares out of the pasture and closed the gate, then pitched the bridle into the long grass under the fence and held out the oats to Dragon.

"Come on, Dragon. You're about to get your first lesson. Lyle's too easy with you. He doesn't understand that a horse has to know who's boss right from the first. He's going to have you so spoiled you won't be good for anything."

Dragon allowed himself to be tied to the fence, since that was necessary to get the oats. But when the girl approached his head, she came not with oats but with the leather-and-metal thing that smelled of the black mare and sweat and wet grass, and woke memories of pain and fear.

He flung his head away from it, but the girl was quick and deft. Dragon felt her thumb slip into the corner of his mouth. It pressed against his tongue and gave off a bitter taste. He twisted his mouth away from it, and instantly the thumb was replaced by the metal bar he feared so deeply. Before he could react, the leather was over his ears and the reins around his neck.

The lead rope was detached from his halter, but the girl held his head hard by the bridle's reins, and she was not so easily shaken off as the boy was. She moved in toward his shoulder, and, suddenly, she was on top of him. Her legs squeezed deep into the flesh of his barrel, and there was a sense of being gathered up that came through the reins and into Dragon's head.

"Easy now; easy, boy." Her voice was firmer than the voice he was used to, but it lacked the boy's soothing quality. It failed to still his rising fear.

The cowboy shouted and waved his arms behind Dragon's eyes, and the snake of pain tightened around his head.

Dragon bolted. Away from the old terrors he fled, eyes wide, legs trembling. A voice followed him, close behind his ears, calling his name with anger and then with echoes of his own fear.

He plunged over the creek and galloped hard up the hill, bucking as he went. Low tree branches broke against his face.

Near the top of the hill his fear began to ebb, and in its place rose a hard, surging pride. The weight on his back was gone. It had not conquered him.

All that remained was the leather that now flapped uselessly around his head. He rubbed the side of his head against a tree until the bridle fell away with an uncomfortable clacking against his teeth. Then he turned to look down the hill behind him.

The girl climbed slowly toward him, holding one elbow. Dragon's instincts told him there was nothing more to be feared from her. He stood his ground and watched her come. She smelled of bruised grass and blood and the salt of tears.

But her voice was close to normal. "Where's my bridle, you old cuss? Oh. There it is. How am I going to explain a busted cheek strap? Or this elbow, for that matter?"

Then she looked up, and Dragon felt the steadiness of her eyes on his.

"I'll say this for you, you old son of a buck.

You're more horse than *I* can handle. If Lyle ever makes any headway with you at all, he's got my respect, boy."

She made a rueful face and turned to leave, then called back over her shoulder, "Of course I'd never admit it to him." She laughed and began making her way stiffly down the hill.

The tension remained in Dragon's head through the afternoon hours, and sent him shying from squirrels and blue jays. When Lyle and Rocky appeared at the pasture gate with the oat bucket, Dragon bolted to the comparative safety of the far side of the creek.

"Come on, Dragon. Got some good old oats for you, buddy."

Dragon watched with widened eyes and began to sweat.

"Dragon? What's the matter?" Lyle frowned and looked from Dragon to Rocky. "I wonder what's wrong with him?"

Rocky shrugged. "He's probably just having an off day. Why don't you leave him alone today, give him a break."

"But why would he act this way, all of a sudden? He was coming along just fine."

"How should I know?" Rocky snapped. "Something spooked him probably."

70

While Rocky was catching and bridling the black mare, using a dusty old bridle of her father's, Lyle stood under the elms and stared thoughtfully at the little freckled stallion across the creek.

"You know, that's right," he said at length, to no one in particular. "How are we supposed to know why an animal acts the way he does, when we don't know all the things that're in his head? I mean, here he is—fifteen years old, and all those years he's been having experiences that I don't know anything about. In his own mind he probably has very good reasons for being afraid of the things he's afraid of. If what he does doesn't seem sensible to me, maybe it's because I don't know the whole story. Right?"

He turned to Rocky, but she was busy adjusting the bridle on Midnight's head. She didn't answer.

Chapter Six

The next morning the girl came and took away the black mare, and the boy came and called and offered the oat pail. Dragon watched from the top of the hill. When Lyle finally gave up and left, Dragon walked down and stood looking over the top of the gate toward the sound of the boy's voice beyond the barn.

The day passed slowly.

The next few mornings the boy came across the pasture and talked to Dragon in his soft bewildered voice. "Come on, Dragon. What's the matter? We were getting along so well. Don't you want to get your neck brushed?"

Dragon maintained a safe distance between himself and the boy in spite of the lure of the oats and the pleasantness of Lyle's voice. Memories of old hurts and humiliations, roused by the girl's bridle, were astir in Dragon's head. The boy seemed harmless, but he was connected in some way with the girl and the bridle, and with the receding but still present memory of the trailer and the hurt in his leg.

And yet after the boy left each day, the pasture seemed somehow lacking. With the black mare gone during the day under the legs of the girl, Dragon had just four placid grazing mares to occupy his energy, and they needed nothing from him. Already they carried the beginnings of his sons and daughters within their smooth flanks. His function was fulfilled. The pasture, though much smaller than his domain in Texas, was many times more lush and protected. The grass was deep, moist, and richly flavored, and supplemented by oats, a large pink salt block, and an ever-full water trough. No jet planes shrieked down out of the skies here, as in Texas—only cars and farm trucks rattling and pinging along the gravel road some distance away. People were closer and more constantly around him in this place, but by now Dragon understood that the mares needed no protection from these people.

His days were long and useless. His years of accumulating skills that kept him and his mares alive in Mexico seemed wasted now, as did the skills. He might race his own shadow, jump the stream, rear up and fight imaginary enemies, but these games were just that. Games. The little stallion grew more and more restless with every empty day that passed.

And in the natural way of things, the boy's morning visits gradually became the most interesting part of Dragon's day. One day in late summer, after evading Lyle's attempts to get close to him, Dragon fell into step behind the discouraged boy as Lyle started to leave. He walked several paces behind the boy, and it took a few minutes for Lyle to realize the horse was following.

Lyle turned. "Dragon."

Dragon stopped when Lyle did, but started walking again when the boy continued. Lyle walked more slowly, looking back over his shoulder and grinning.

At the spot under the trees where they used to have their sitting sessions, Dragon allowed the gap between them to close. He came to Lyle slowly but steadily.

"Dragon, old buddy, I can't believe it. I wish I knew what was going on in your head, horse."

Dragon cautiously extended his head toward the oats bucket. He had missed the delicious stuff. He lipped up a scoop of the slithery grains and tongued them back into his mouth, while the boy's hand rubbed his neck, lifted the hot weight of his mane to let the breeze cool him.

When the oats were gone and there was nothing to taste but the bottom of the bucket, Dragon felt the boy's hand on his halter, felt the snap of the lead rope beneath his chin. He tensed.

"There's a good old Dragon horse; you don't have anything to be afraid of, so don't get silly."

The boy's voice had the same soothing effect it used to have. Dragon relaxed.

"I tell you what," Lyle murmured. "Let's have a little practice at being led. We're going to have to get you used to that before we can do any real training, okay?"

Lyle began to stroll along the fence, his left hand gripping the lead rope, his right arm draped over Dragon's neck so the petting could continue. It seemed the natural thing for Dragon to do, falling into step beside the boy. They walked down a shady corridor between the fence and a row of large old shade trees. Dragon walked this way often himself, while watching and listening toward the buildings. It was pleasant now, walking along beside the boy, having his mane lifted off the hot side of his neck, getting the itchy place behind his ears rubbed, listening to the soft voice.

The boy halted and said, "Whoa."

Dragon stopped, because the boy did.

"Good boy, Dragon, good old buddy."

Dragon swiveled an ear toward the boy. The

warmth of praise was something he had never before heard in a voice. He didn't understand it, but it made him feel mildly good.

"Gee-up, Dragon."

The walk resumed. At the corner of the fence Lyle pulled gently at the halter to turn Dragon around, but suddenly Dragon no longer felt like walking beside the boy. The uphill slope invited him to gallop up it. He planted his feet and pulled his head free from the weight of the boy. The flapping lead rope slapped against his neck and shoulders as he bucked and cantered up the hill, weaving among the trees, swaying his body from side to side as he changed leads for the sharp turns around the tree trunks.

At the top of the hill he stopped and turned to look for the boy. Lyle was far below, standing stiffly at the fence corner and looking up at him.

Dragon felt a faint regret that the boy was not still with him, but he forgot it when the bay mare sauntered over to graze beside him.

Through the weeks that followed, Dragon's mornings were broken and brightened by the lessons with the boy. The sessions began with oats and brushing while Dragon stood tied to the fence. By now the brushing extended all the way down his legs, even the injured leg, which was scarred but no longer painful. The damaged hoof was rounded out nearly as fully as its mate, to the constant delight of the veterinarian, who never failed to look at it and scratch his head on his visits to the farm.

The lessons, if they could be called that, took up the sitting routine again, with Lyle perched quietly on Dragon's back while the horse remained tied to the fence. Then Dragon accompanied Lyle on increasingly longer walks around the pasture. Sometimes the walks ended with Dragon simply getting tired and running away; sometimes they ended with Lyle releasing him and pouring praises into Dragon's ears. More and more often, as Lyle learned to read the small signs of Dragon's discontent, the lessons were halted under Lyle's control.

While they walked, the words "whoa" and "gee-up" seemed to occur regularly in connection with stopping and starting. One day, on hearing the word "whoa" and expecting the boy to halt, Dragon came to a stop. Immediately Lyle poured a gentle torrent of praise and happiness into Dragon's ears. The little horse listened and puzzled and felt oddly happy.

Days later, Dragon began to notice that Lyle was walking farther back, about level with his shoulder, and that the lead rope, which was now two lead ropes knotted around his neck, pressed against his neck when the boy turned in one direction or the other. Rather than pushing or pulling at Dragon's head as he used to, the boy was now attempting to press Dragon's neck to one side or the other to get the horse into a turn. It was easy enough to overpower the boy and go on walking in his own direction, and Dragon often did just that, but this sometimes meant walking into a fence or a tree or taking a rougher path than the one the boy was attempting to force him onto.

It took only a short time for Dragon to realize the connection between the neck pressure and the boy's desire to turn him, but he resented Lyle's infringement on his freedom. If the neck pressure came at a time when Dragon himself wanted to turn, he allowed himself to bend with the boy's leaning. If not, Dragon simply chose his own path and stiffened his neck against the ropes.

Days and nights became cooler in Dragon's pasture. The grass took on a crisper, drier flavor, and often, early in the morning, it was frosted silver until the sun came up. Leaves drifted down under Dragon's trees, and the lessons changed from mornings to late afternoons.

The boy began slipping a halterlike thing onto Dragon's head during their walks. At its introduction Dragon stiffened, but it contained no metal to be forced into his mouth, only an additional layer of straps about his head and a second set of ropes, these of braided leather, around his neck. It did not seem a threatening addition to the halter and lead rope, especially since the boy continued to use the halter and lead rope for such controls as he was able to implement with Dragon.

Dragon was not aware of the change when Lyle began guiding him with pressure from the hackamore's reins rather than the halter rope.

One day Lyle said, "We're going to have to graduate you to the barn lot, old buddy. It's time I got on with the real riding, and frankly you've got too much room out here to run away with me."

The pasture gate swung open, and for the first time since spring Dragon was out of the familiar field. He felt mildly uneasy as he pranced up the short hill to the barn lot, and, hardly knowing he was doing so, he drew confidence from the fact that Lyle was beside his shoulder, steadying his head with the pressure of the reins and with his smooth familiar voice.

Then they were inside the small circle of the barn lot. The barn door and the lot gate were closed. There was nothing here but a circle of churned grassless earth with high fences around it.

That first day they did nothing more than the usual walking and sitting. In his uneasiness at the strange surroundings Dragon followed the boy closely as they circled and doubled back and walked in figure-eights.

Toward the end of the lesson Dragon's heart was set to pounding by the rattling approach of a car. It came toward the fence somewhere on the far side, where he couldn't see it, but it stopped before it got threateningly close, and its noise died. He took a deep breath and relaxed his neck and ears.

Mr. Hunter's head appeared over the fence top. The man watched quietly, leaning his city-suited arms along the splintery top of the fence.

"He's coming right along, isn't he?" Mr. Hunter said when Lyle tied Dragon to the fence and began to brush him.

The boy turned and grinned. "I thought I'd better start working him up here when I start riding him. You don't think Mom will care, do you? About my riding him?"

"Well, it's like we told you last summer, Lyle. You've got enough good sense not to take foolish chances with him, the way Rocky probably would. Just use your head, that's all. He certainly doesn't seem to be a mean horse by nature, does he?"

"Oh, no, Dad. He's never done anything deliberately *to* me, like kicking or biting or anything like that, and he's gotten so I can walk right up to him in the pasture and catch him, and he leads pretty well."

"I'd say you were making good headway with him then."

"Yes, but he's kind of funny, Dad. I don't know. He's smart—he's awfully smart in fact—and he learns the commands fast, but he doesn't seem to care whether he *does* them or not. If I try to turn him, he might turn, or he might take off up the hill and I'll have to play tag with him half the afternoon to get the hackamore off of him."

"Hmm." Mr. Hunter thought for a moment and said, "Well, you have to remember, this is no pliable little yearling colt you're trying to teach. This is a fifteen-year-old stallion who's spent most of those fifteen years being his own boss and the leader of a herd. I suppose he feels the same way I would if I had to go back to being a junior law clerk with someone always telling me what to do, after twenty years of running my own law firm."

Lyle stopped brushing and stared at his father. "You know, I never thought of it that way."

Mr. Hunter turned toward the house. "Better put him away and get washed up. I expect it's about suppertime."

Chapter Seven

The next day in the barn lot, Lyle eased up onto Dragon's back and then slowly leaned forward and unsnapped the rope that held Dragon to the fence. Dragon felt his neck being pushed to the side by the reins; he felt the tightening of the boy's thigh muscles and heard, "Gee-up, Dragon."

He stood, confused. That word was supposed to mean walking with the boy beside him, but the boy was on top of him instead.

"Gee-up, old buddy."

The reins pressed harder, turning his head away from the fence. Dragon took a tentative step.

"Good boy, that's the way."

He felt the boy's weight shifting unsteadily on

his back, smelled just the faintest whiff of fear sweat from Lyle's hands. He stopped, confused.

"Gee-up."

Dragon stepped out again and found he could walk around the barn lot with the boy balanced atop him and nothing bad happened. It was an odd sensation, different from when the girl rode him, or the man, years ago, in Mexico. This time there was no pain at his mouth, no attempt to force him into one direction or another. This was little more than just walking with the boy. Lyle's voice came from farther back and higher up, but it was the same reassuring voice, accompanied by the same calming pressure of fingers rubbing his neck, and after the first moment the fear smell went away.

For several days the riding continued. They circled the lot at a walk, going first one direction, then the other, doing a few broad turns and occasional "whoas" and "gee-ups." Because the barn lot offered little in the way of temptation to do otherwise, Dragon allowed himself to be stopped and started and turned. He found pleasure in the warmth of the boy's voice when he responded to the controlling words and pressures, and yet there were deep reservations within the little stallion's mind. Dragon was fully aware, at all times, that his strength was much greater than the boy's and that, just as he often had leaped out from under the mortal mount of a wildcat on his back, he could topple the boy from his back—and with far greater ease. The boy had no claws to bury in Dragon's flesh, very little real balance, and no grip at all.

One afternoon when the boy finished brushing him, a saddle came into Dragon's sight. It was a stock saddle like the one inflicted on him in Mexico, smaller and less ornate but with the same smell and carrying the same frightening meaning. Dragon flattened his ears and struck out at the saddle with his teeth as it came close, on the boy's arm. His teeth raked the leather of the stirrup skirts.

"Take it easy, Dragon. This isn't going to hurt you."

Dragon glared at the boy.

The saddle approached again. Again Dragon drove it away. His heart was pounding.

"Come on, Dragon. Don't be that way. Look. I've got to graduate you from just going around in circles in the barn lot, old buddy, and to be honest, I'm not a good enough rider to stay on you, bareback, if you decide to dump me. So let's even up the odds a little, okay?"

When the saddle approached a third time, Dragon plunged away from it, broke his halter, and galloped around the lot in trembling fear and freedom. It took Lyle most of the afternoon to calm him sufficiently for a brief riding session. Bareback.

Lyle took on a different look as the days passed. He grew more bulky in outline as he walked across the pasture to meet Dragon, and he smelled of leather and wool and fleece. His hands became large and leathery, and his body smells came through more faintly. Dragon himself took on a thicker silhouette as his coat went from sleek and silky to long and shaggy, and he changed from a small neat horse into a large furry pony.

A few days after the saddling failure Lyle mounted Dragon in the pasture rather than leading him up to the barn lot.

"You're going to have to learn to be ridden someplace outside that lot," Lyle muttered as he settled into Dragon's shaggy back. "And I guess this is about as good a place to be thrown as anywhere. Gee-up."

They walked along the fence.

"That's a good old boy. See now. There's nothing hard about that, is there?"

Dragon bobbed his head in rhythm with his clopping hooves as he carried the boy the length of the fence and back again. He felt exhilarated by the cold air coming into his head, and he liked having the boy up there talking into his ears and matching the sway of his light body with the shifting of his own weight as he walked. Dragon tucked his chin up tight to his chest and went into a slow-motion trot, no faster than his walk but offering more release for his high spirits.

"Easy. Whoa, Dragon."

They had veered away from the fence and were approaching the creek at the foot of the hill. As he always did here, Dragon broke into a canter that extended itself into a needlessly high jump over the creek, and then, his exhilaration mounting, he galloped up the hill.

The boy was no longer on his back.

He stopped and looked down the hill. The boy was rising from the depression of the creek, rubbing one shoulder and looking angrily at Dragon.

"Dang you! If you were going to throw me in the creek, why'd you wait till it was frozen over?"

Lyle came close and gathered the hackamore's reins. Dragon sensed pain in the boy, just as he used to sense pain or sickness in his colts, back when the well-being of his colts was his responsibility. The boy's pain was lightly disturbing to Dragon. He extended his nose and smelled at Lyle's jacket. The boy rubbed his gloved hand under Dragon's mane with a new tenderness.

"You didn't mean to dump me, did you? I don't think you care whether I ride you or not. You don't seem to mind my being on your back, but I wonder if I'm ever going to have any control over you. You *know* what I want already; you just don't know yet that you *have* to do it."

Lyle climbed onto Dragon's back with a small muttered "ouch," and the lesson began again.

Every afternoon, in the narrowing slice of time between Lyle's arrival home on the yellow school bus and the falling of darkness, Dragon carried the boy back and forth along the fence and among the trees in the lower part of the pasture. They avoided the creek. As they grew more accustomed to each other in this new relationship, Dragon's feelings about the riding swung more firmly from distrust to enjoyment. Except for this hour, his day was un-eventful, so the riding made a pleasant break in his time.

The only times Dragon didn't like were those moments when the boy attempted to control him. When the pressure on his nose from the hackamore became severe, Dragon tightened into rebellion. He reared or bolted for a few steps, or bucked a bit, and then the boy would be walking toward him, limping or holding an elbow and talking in an angry or hurt voice.

When the snow came, the pasture and barn lot gates were propped open so that Dragon and the mares could stand in the shelter of the barn. One half of the barn was an open area built for cattle to mill in during bad weather. The wind was off the mares in there, and the hay bunk was kept full. The mares were growing full-flanked and placid now, and they were content to stand and doze inside the barn. Dragon divided his time between the pasture, which he preferred, and the barn, where the mares were.

One day while Lyle was riding him near the pasture gate, Dragon heard a mare squeal angrily. He turned and broke into a canter, intent on driving the squabbling mares apart before an angry squeal developed into an angry kick in the flanks and an injured foal. Keeping peace among pregnant mares was one of the few jobs left to him now.

But the boy was fighting him, trying to keep him from the mares.

"Whoa, Dragon. Whoa."

The hackamore became a vise around the bones of Dragon's face as Lyle threw all his strength against the reins. Dragon shook his head angrily from side to side. His neck arched. His ears lay flat against his head. All of the pride of a herd stallion rose in rebellion against the boy's interference.

He plunged up the hill and into the barn, where the two bay mares glared their hostility at each other. Dragon snorted his way between them and, by his dominating presence, settled them back into a sullen

calm. The boy was still atop him, emitting pulsations of fear.

Rocky's face appeared beyond the hay bunk. "Hey, Lyle, are you riding him or is he riding you?"

"Oh. You scared me. I didn't know you were there. Well, I'll tell you, right now it's about fifty-fifty. He goes where I want him to if he was planning on going that way anyhow. Otherwise I can either go along for the ride or fall off."

She chuckled, then got serious. "You know what you're doing, don't you? You're spoiling him, and you're never going to get him broke if you let him get away with stuff like that. You know as well as I do, the horse has to *know* you're the boss, right from the first, or the whole thing is hopeless."

Dragon moved to the hay bunk and began to eat.

Rocky went on. "Look at how I did with Midnight when I was breaking her. I never hurt her or anything, but I never once let her get away with disobeying a command once she knew what the command meant, and look how nice she turned out. If she started acting up, I cracked down on her, right then. You have to, Lyle."

He sighed. "I know. You're right. It's just that Dragon is different."

"A horse is a horse is a horse."

"Yeah, but Dragon is fifteen years old, Rock.

Like Dad said, you can't expect him to take to train-ing the way a colt would. Dragon has this kind of, well, pride. Heck, he's led a whole life that we don't know anything about. We don't know what kind of mistreatment or bad experiences he might have had. He can't talk and tell us."

"Well, that's true."

"I just feel he needs more patience than a colt would, in learning all this stuff. I have to get him to *want* to obey the commands. He's not going to do it any other way."

"Maybe. I know one thing, though. You've got to quit trying to ride him around the other horses. Get him off by himself, around the house or out where I've got my practice barrels, and I'll bet he'd be more willing to let you do the steering. He wouldn't be so sure of himself in strange territory."

The boy said nothing.

The next afternoon Lyle led Dragon through a small side gate in the lot fence, then mounted. Rocky stood a respectful distance away, watching. With tightly pricked ears Dragon sidestepped around the corner of the barn. His eyes were filled with new shapes—the huge red square of the farmhouse, snow-laden trees and shrubs, heaps of white that might be hiding anything.

The boy's voice and hands and legs urged him

forward, and since the place was strange to him, Dragon found himself following Lyle's directions. Uneasily, suspicious of what might be under the snow, Dragon did a slow dance along the car tracks of the lane. Then, when Lyle pressed his neck to the left, he moved onto the buried grass of the lawn and made a circle around the house. At one point Lyle waved at the woman who stood in the large picture window, and she waved back.

They went around the house once more, then did a figure-eight across the dead vegetable garden. Dragon followed the pressure of the reins. He was too busy watching out for dangers to object to Lyle's guidance.

Something curious and disturbing began to move in the depth of Dragon's understanding. Connections were almost made, then wavered away.

"Take him up the lane and back, why don't you?" Rocky called. "He's doing great."

At the car tracks Lyle leaned Dragon to the left. They moved up the long lane toward the road at a dancing half-trot.

Dragon was about to settle into a walk when suddenly headlights flashed around the corner and began moving slowly toward him. The old memories seared his brain.

The trucks roared at him with their headlights boring into his eyes, and the mares screamed and

died, and one truck hit him, broke him, sent him
swimming into pain.

"Easy, Dragon. It's just Dad's car. He's stopped.
It won't hurt you."

Heart pounding, legs trembling, Dragon backed
frantically away from the lights. The boy's legs beat
on his sides, the reins pushed hard against his neck
in an effort to force him back onto the lane, but
Dragon was rigid with terror.

He backed faster. Suddenly there was no hardness under the snow. His legs sank; he toppled over
backward and rolied.

After a dizzy instant he climbed to his feet and
shook himself off. The boy lay in the snow. Dragon
took a step forward and thrust his head down between Mr. Hunter and Rocky as they knelt beside
Lyle. A sense of pain came up in great waves from
the boy. Dragon dropped his muzzle to the boy's
cheek and smelled salty tears.

Chapter Eight

Days passed, and the boy didn't come for their afternoon rides. The disturbed, uneasy feeling that the
boy's pain had lodged in Dragon stayed with the
horse and grew as the days went by. Late afternoon
meant that the boy was supposed to come and get
him and put the hackamore on and sit on his back
and go with him. But the boy didn't come.

Dragon watched at the barn lot gate every
afternoon until well past dark and then wandered
back to the mares, oddly disappointed. The girl
came every day to feed and water him and the mares,
but she didn't rub behind his ears or talk to him
or sit on his back in the undemanding way that the
boy used to.

One afternoon Dragon began feeling that the

boy was not far away, on the other side of the barn. He galloped around the lot, readied himself, then leaped the fence. Around the barn he trotted, stopping to get his bearings.

It was the other big red building that seemed to contain the boy. Head high, nostrils searching for Lyle's smell, Dragon danced toward the house. Just as he had on that other day, he circled the house slowly, looking toward it, listening and smelling.

Suddenly he saw Lyle. The boy was sitting beyond the big window. At first Dragon was puzzled because Lyle seemed to be giving off no scent. Then he heard the voice, and he was sure.

"Hey, Dragon!"

He moved toward the house, stepping carefully up onto the low porch that separated him from the window. He didn't like the feel of the hollow wood beneath his feet, but he was compelled forward by a rushing new emotion. He had felt only passing glimmers of it before—when the boy praised him, and once in Texas when Mr. Burr had somehow saved him from the slaughter of the truck's headlights, and in moments so far back in his memory that they left only traces of traces. It was the way he might have felt toward his mares and colts, had they not been so heavily his responsibility.

He clopped across the porch and pressed his muzzle against the glass.

"Hey, Mom, come and help me out on the porch." The boy's voice was vibrant with joy. "I have a visitor."

A few moments later Lyle was standing unsteadily on the porch with his arms around Dragon's neck. One of the boy's legs had become huge and white and stiff. Mrs. Hunter steadied Lyle from behind and struggled to keep a jacket over his shoulders.

"How'd he get out of the fence?" she asked.

"Must have jumped, I guess. He was worried about me, weren't you, old buddy?"

Mrs. Hunter snorted.

"You didn't have to worry, Dragon," Lyle said as he rubbed Dragon's neck. "It's just a little broken ankle and some bruised ribs. You didn't mean to hurt me—I know that."

"You can add pneumonia to the list if you don't get back into the house right now." Mrs. Hunter steered Lyle through the door, then shooed Dragon into the barn.

After that Lyle hobbled to the barn to visit Dragon for at least a few minutes every day. Rocky joined him one afternoon.

"Mom says if you're well enough to go to the barn, you're well enough to go to school," she said as she settled beside Lyle on the hay bunk. Dragon stood dozing with his head close to the boy's knee.

"I know it. She says it every day," Lyle said. "I'll probably have to start back Monday. What I want to know is how soon I can start riding again."

"You want to start riding again?" Rocky raised her eyebrows.

"Sure. What did you think?"

She shrugged. "I don't know. I figured you wouldn't want to mess around with Dragon any more after that fall."

Lyle reached for a strand of Dragon's mane. "That wasn't his fault, really. The car spooked him, and he backed off the edge of the ditch, was all."

Lyle's eyes were on Dragon; he didn't see the look of grudging respect on Rocky's face.

During the following weeks, while he was unable to ride, Lyle renewed his efforts to accustom Dragon to the saddle. Every day he laid the saddle in the hay bunk, closer and closer to where Dragon was tied for his daily brushing and visiting sessions. Dragon distrusted the saddle, but it did nothing more than lie there day after day.

About the time Dragon decided the saddle was not a threat after all, Lyle lifted it and brought it toward Dragon's shoulder. Dragon bit at it. It stopped, but didn't move away. The boy kept talking in a tone that meant there was nothing to worry about. The saddle moved closer. Dragon stiffened, but still the boy's voice told him it was all right.

The saddle came to rest on Dragon's back. He stiffened even more and began to sweat, listening to the stream of reassuring words with all his strength. Then the saddle was gone, and nothing bad had happened.

Within a week Dragon was standing calmly while Lyle settled the saddle on his back and brought the cinch up snugly behind Dragon's elbows.

Soon after that came the afternoon when Lyle led the fully saddled Dragon out the front door of the barn and mounted him. Dragon stood tensely, feeling the difference between boy and saddle and just boy. Lyle's weight was farther back now, and the saddle was a stiff barrier between Dragon's muscles and the boy's, so that Dragon could no longer sense which way Lyle was going to lean. And yet there was a solidity and a sureness to the boy's manner that Dragon had not felt before. The sureness was something Dragon could lean into and brace himself against.

He felt the touch of Lyle's heels against his ribs and a gentle pressure of reins against the side of his neck. From some deep part of his mind came a wave of pride, pride that he understood what the boy wanted him to do. He stepped out.

They made a slow circle around the house. At first the creaking of the saddle bothered Dragon, but then it seemed a harmless sound, and he forgot about it.

They approached a clothesline pole. Lyle steered him around it. A cat crossed in front of them, and again the pressure of the reins on his neck steered Dragon around the possible danger of the small glaring animal.

Lyle turned him away from the house, straight toward a drift of snow higher than the few inches that covered the lawn. Dragon wanted to veer away from the drift, but Lyle's legs and hands told him to go straight into it. He balked.

"Go on, Dragon. It's all right."

Again the boy urged him into the drift. Cautiously he placed a hoof through the snow. Solid ground met him. He walked forward, through the drift, unhurt.

Suddenly the small pieces of understanding that had begun to gather the day of Lyle's fall were floating to the surface of Dragon's mind. The guiding hands of his rider were not a threat. They were safety.

The boy knew things that Dragon didn't know, and when Lyle sat on Dragon's back and showed him which way to move, there was nothing to fear from the strange shapes and movements that came at him in this unfamiliar world.

The boy knew.

Dragon arched his neck and set his head so that Lyle's hands on the reins seemed to carry him along. He did a slow sideways dance that did not unbalance the boy but only expressed the exploding warmth within him.

Chapter Nine

There were five days that spring when Lyle and Dragon did not go riding, the days when each of the mares foaled. Then the barn was rich with the smell and excitement of foaling, and Dragon was full of remembered wildness. On those days Lyle wisely left him alone.

But when the foaling was finished, Dragon was glad to resume the afternoon rides. These foals were surrounded by people, by stall walls, by all the security a newborn horse could need. There was nothing Dragon could do for them, and he sensed this with an emptiness that made him look forward to the boy's coming each afternoon.

Through snow, then mud, then succulent new grass they trotted or cantered, around the farm buildings, up the lane as far as the road. Then one day Lyle came for Dragon in the morning rather than at the customary late-afternoon time.

"It's summer vacation, Dragon," the boy said as he settled the saddle in place and reached under Dragon's ribs for the cinch. "Now we start the real work. I've got big plans for you, old buddy."

Dragon bucked just the smallest hop of a buck as he danced up the bank toward the barn. The sun was hot enough to make a Mexican mustang feel good all the way to the middle of his bones. They circled the barn and trotted past the house, around the clothesline pole, and into the small flat field between the house yard and the road.

The reins touched Dragon's neck, guiding him toward a triangle of rusted oil barrels. He stiffened his ears and stared at the barrels. Something about their smell made him think of trucks. He hesitated, but the boy's legs urged him on. Another few steps and he was surrounded by the barrels, one ahead of him, one on either side. His heart began to pound.

"It's all right. They're just barrels. They can't hurt you."

Lyle's legs pushed him forward until the front barrel was within reach of his nose. Then, mercifully, came the pressure of the hackamore on his nose, telling him to stop. He halted, stretched his head toward the barrel, touched it. It rocked. He leaped aside.

The moment of fear passed as quickly as it came, but it left Lyle sprawled on the ground. Dragon looked around at the boy in mild surprise.

"It's all right, Dragon," said Lyle, a bit breathless, picking himself up and dusting off his jeans. "You didn't hurt me. I just wasn't prepared for that jump."

With Lyle back in place in the saddle, they began circling the barrels, first at a walk and then faster as Dragon ceased to stare and stiffen his ears at the smelly obstacles.

"Okay, I think we'll let that rest for a while, and try the poles."

Dragon slowed to a walk and followed the pressure of the reins, across the field toward a row of very tall slim poles. This was uncertain territory, and he was willing to let the boy choose the way.

"The point of the game," Lyle said, stroking Dragon's neck to the gentle swaying rhythm of the horse's walk, "is to weave between the poles, all the way to the end, and then turn around as fast as you can and weave back to the starting line. You have to do it at a dead gallop, which means you'll have to change your leads about every two steps or you'll get your feet tangled up and fall on your nose. It's the same general idea as the barrel racing except for the different pattern. We'll start out slow, okay?"

They zigzagged through the line of poles at a walk, then a trot. The poles held no threatening smells, as the oil barrels had; they were simply a row of uniform branchless young trees, and Dragon had spent a lifetime dodging among trees. He flicked his tail and increased his speed.

"Easy now. We'd better go slow at first."

Dragon shook his head in an unknowingly appropriate gesture of impatience and rocked into a canter. By this time they had made several trips up and down the row of poles, and Dragon continued the weaving pattern, faster and faster.

"Whoa, Dragon."

Exhilaration filled the little stallion. Not since he had played coltish games with the other yearlings in the Den of the Dragons Canyon had he felt this sense of enjoyment in the motion of his body.

The weight on his back began to shift to one side, and instinctively Dragon moved under the weight to restore its balance. The boy. The boy was with him. He slowed to a gentle canter, and then, when the reins asked it of him, he stopped.

The boy's hand was warm on his neck, and it trembled.

"Dragon, you know something? You are going

to be some super gaming horse. If only I can keep from falling off on those sharp turns! Whew."

Every day after that, in the early morning hours before the sun grew hot, Dragon and Lyle worked out in the little field. At first they just followed the patterns around barrels and poles; then gradually Lyle began asking for refinements—closer turns, faster starts, sudden stops.

Not since Dragon had lived free in the Mexican mountains had he been called on to move with such speed and precision. Then it had been a matter of survival, of dodging mountain lions and battling marauding stallions and striking at snakes that threatened a sleeping foal. Now he danced and charged and swerved for the joy of the movements and for the odd feeling of satisfaction that came over him as he combined his power with the boy's skilled guidance.

One day Rocky rode into the training field on a strange horse, a large sorrel gelding borrowed from a friend. Dragon snorted up to the horse, realized he was not a threat, and settled down again.

Lyle grinned at Rocky. "I think he's going to be all right with strange horses, don't you?"

Rocky shrugged. "This one is easy, though. He's a gelding. You still don't know how he'll be with mares, and especially with other stallions."

Lyle looked away. "I know it. Let's race. Down to the fence and back. Ready. Set. Go!"

Dragon sensed the race even before he felt the urging of Lyle's body. He stretched his neck and flattened himself to the ground and ran as though his life still depended on raw speed, as it once had. At the fence he churned to a stop, spun, held himself for an instant while Lyle regained his balance, then raced back home again, ridiculously far ahead of the other horse.

He pranced and arched his neck proudly when it was over. This was a new element, this feeling of competition with another horse. The solitary riding, the weaving and churning and bending with Lyle's shifting weight, had been deeply satisfying, but now that the boy was asking him to prove his superiority over other horses, Dragon felt a rightness, a completeness, he had not known since people came into his life.

He gloried in it.

All morning, until the sun grew too hot, the two horses and their riders worked among the barrels and poles. They raced singly now, going one at a time around the barrels and among the poles, but the feeling of the race stayed with Dragon. He outdid himself.

When Lyle and Rocky finally reined the horses

in near the gate, Lyle said, "I'm going to do it! I'm going to get him in the International, by golly! If Dad will let me. Dragon is just too darned good not to be appreciated by the whole world. Don't you think he's great?"

Rocky nodded. "He looked good today—I'll say that for him. But, Lyle, don't forget he's a sixteen-year-old horse, and he's little compared to what his competition will be. And he's green. Do you realize how many shows he would have to enter, and win, this summer, just to qualify for competition at the International Championship? That would be asking an awful, awful lot of a young horse, much less one Dragon's age."

"I know it. But he can do it."

"How about the Indian costume classes you'd have to ride him in, with no bridle or anything, just that little skinny rawhide loop around his jaw? You realize there are going to be other stallions in those costume classes? Do you honestly think you can control him that well?"

"Sure. Maybe."

They sat silently, staring off into the summer heat haze. Dragon turned his head around and bumped the boy's toe with his nose. Standing still bored him.

"Rocky?"

"What?"

Lyle hesitated for a moment. "Do you want to ride Dragon for a little while?"

She stared at him in quick surprise, then looked away. "No, that's okay. I'll stick with old Pepper here. But thanks anyway."

"What's the matter—you afraid of him?"

"Well, hardly," she answered stiffly. "I'm just not sure you could handle Pepper, that's all. And the Johnsons might not like me letting other people ride him."

"Oh."

Lyle lifted the reins and set Dragon at a slow jog toward the barrels. There was a smile in his voice when he whispered, "I think she *is* afraid of you, Dragon."

Chapter Ten

Dragon woke, startled. It was deep night and even darker than night-dark under the trees at the top of the pasture hill. He turned his head and listened for the sound that woke him. A swish through the grass by the creek. A movement.

With a warning snort, a dash, he gathered the five mares and their sleepy babies into a circle, then placed himself between them and the approaching shape.

"Dragon."

It was the boy. Dragon relaxed and moved down the slope to meet him.

"Hi, old buddy. Did I wake you up? I'm supposed to be in bed myself, but I couldn't sleep. Dad says you can have your chance at being a show horse,

111

Dragon. *If* I can control you, and *if* it doesn't wear you out too much. Mom worried about me being a good enough rider and you being too old, but Dad finally gave in and said we could try."

The boy was standing close to Dragon's neck, fiddling with his mane. Dragon lowered his head and rubbed one ear up and down, hard, against Lyle's chest. It felt good.

"The thing is, now that I've won the argument, I'm scared I *won't* be able to handle you. I wish there was some way I could talk to you and make you understand what I'm saying. You're standing there like an old plow horse now, but you and I both know that when I'm riding you, you only do what I ask because you want to, not because you're obeying me."

Lyle sat down with his back against a tree trunk, and Dragon moved close and grazed around the boy's feet.

"You know what? I just realized. I really don't want you to obey me. It scares the daylights out of me sometimes when I'm riding you and I feel all that power, and know I can't control it, and yet I think the reason I love you so much is that you *are* stronger than I am. We're not just obedient horse and all-powerful master, like Midnight and Rocky. We're more like—like partners, and I think, this way, we can kind of respect each other."

Lyle was silent for a long time. Then he stood and pulled a wad of baling twine out of his jeans pocket.

"Dragon, we're going to try something. I decided if you're going to be uncontrollable with an Indian loop, I'd rather find it out now, when nobody can see us, than in the show ring when we'll be in front of hundreds of people, and with other stallions nearby."

In among the wad of grass in his mouth Dragon suddenly found a band of something soft, narrow, prickly, tasteless. It went snugly around his bottom jaw and carried messages of the boy's movements, as the hackamore reins did. He moved uneasily as Lyle jumped onto his back.

"Gee-up, Dragon."

He opened his mouth and tried to work his tongue out from under the twine. The boy was pressing him to the left, away from the mares and colts. He didn't want to leave them, not in the middle of the night, not with only this flimsy thing in his mouth through which to depend on the boy. He danced sideways a step or two; then, when Lyle's balance became unsteady on his back, he stopped dancing, settled into a flat walk, and moved down the hill, away from the mares.

The boy slid off to lead him through the pasture gate, and then remounted. Dragon neighed uneasily toward the mares, barely visible now at the far end of the pasture. The muscles of the boy's legs sent tremors of nervousness through Dragon, as did the scent of Lyle's fear-triggered perspiration.

Dragon sidestepped up the slope and around the barn. So far nothing bad was happening, although the house and shrubs and parked cars looked different in the sharply etched moon-shadows. Down the lane they went, sometimes walking, sometimes at the slow-motion trot that was Dragon's way of saying he wanted to run. They turned onto the gravel road toward town.

"See, Dragon, you have to learn how to do this because we're going to try to make an International Champion out of you at the POA show this fall, and part of what you'll have to do is compete in the Indian costume class, which means riding you without a saddle or bridle, with only a leather thong around your jaw, just like the Indians did."

Lyle needed the reassuring sound of his own voice as much as Dragon did. He talked on.

"First we'll have to take you to every horse show we can get to, all summer, and you'll have to win, or place high, in a whole lot of things like barrel races and pole bending and regular pleasure classes and trail classes, where you have to go over bridges and into trailers and have plastic raincoats flapped at you, without getting scared.

"Then at the big show there'll be POA ponies from all over the world, lots of them your kids and grandkids, and you're going to have to win against all of them. Everybody thinks I'm crazy. I guess I probably am."

While the boy's voice went on, Dragon began enjoying the ride. As a young colt in the mountains, he had loved traveling by moonlight, shying playfully at the deep black shadows and dodging kicks from the old stallion who was his sire.

As he grew older, an element of loneliness had come into his life. He was obliged to drive off the old stallion and the stud colts of his own age in order to attain leadership of the herd. After that there had been no romps in the night air with other colts. Dignity and watchfulness, these were two of the necessities of his life then; without them he would have been killed.

Now, years and miles away from his coltish romps in the Den of the Dragons Canyon, he felt again the urge to prance and plunge and shake his head at the world. The loneliness of a leader, a loneliness that had so long been a part of him that he hardly knew it existed, began to lift and float away.

The boy was here.

The boy was perched, none too steadily, on Dragon's back, telling him when to go left or right to find the smoothest part of the road, talking to him. Being with him.

Dragon pranced, but he pranced so smoothly and gently that Lyle's balance was not swayed.

When they came to the highway, the boy asked that he go along the side of it, reassured him that it was all right. A car approached. Dragon halted, staring into the headlights, his neck rigid, his heart hammering.

"It's all right, Dragon. It's just a car. It won't hurt you."

The boy's voice sounded calm. Dragon fastened onto the stream of words, leaned into the boy's presence.

The car whooshed past. Dragon relaxed in a flush of heat, and moved forward on shaky but steadying legs. The boy's voice was warm with praise. Dragon's neck arched a bit, and his enjoyment of the night came back in full strength.

"See, that wasn't so bad, was it?"

Suddenly a mammoth livestock truck roared into Dragon's vision from behind, coming up close at his side. The old terror filled his head, but this time the boy's voice cut through it, held him in the present. His eyes saw, not the glaring headlights and the slaughtered mares on a Texas highway, but the gentle green trough of a roadside ditch in Iowa. The truck rushed past him in a blast of noise, and the

116

wind from it lifted his mane. But the truck did not touch him. The boy's voice had kept it away.

The ditch became lawn as houses moved in on either side of them. When the twine against his neck asked him to move onto the paved street, Dragon accepted the suggestion. His hooves made a hollow sound against the concrete, and the hardness of it tingled up the bones of his legs. There were cars here, but they sat motionless along the edge of the street.

A dog came out and barked furiously at Dragon's side, but he knew, even without the reassurances Lyle gave him, that the animal planned to stay beyond the range of his hooves. He snorted and arched his neck in an arrogant display, and the dog retired to its porch.

Through long blocks of houses and then larger, closer buildings, Dragon and his rider walked, passing an occasional moving car or truck. They circled the town square, where Dragon left hoofprints in the soft earth around the bandstand. Then back again among the downtown buildings, along the rows of houses and lawns and parked cars, until the last of the houses was behind them and the long grass of the highway ditch brushed against Dragon's legs.

The sky was turning apple green and pink as they left the highway for the road home. When their farm buildings came into sight, Lyle pressed Dragon off of the road and through an open gate into a hillside cornfield. Terraced strips of grass, yards wide, curved among the rows of corn, a carpet of welcome rolling toward the sunrise.

Dragon quickened his speed.

"Whoa, Dragon," the boy called.

Dragon slowed, but only slightly.

"Oh, okay. Let's go."

Dragon ran, ran for the joy of the speed and the wind in his face and the ground jolting against his hooves.

The boy stayed on his back, and he was glad.

Afterword

In the fall of 1961, at the Third Annual International Pony of the Americas Championship Show, a small, freckled stallion called Dragon was named an International Performance Champion.

In the audience a large, red-faced man with a Texas drawl scratched his head and said, "Well, I'll be dipped."

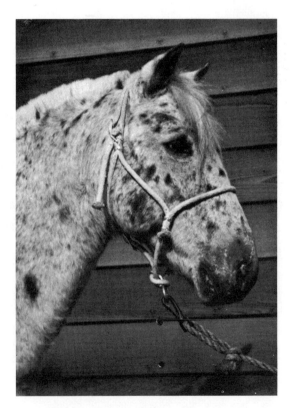

Taken at approximately age 18

About Dragon

No one knows for certain the origin of the Mexican mustangs, small horses that live in the Sierra Madre Mountains in Michoacán, Mexico. But the generally accepted belief is that they originated from a handful of Spanish Barb horses that were being brought to Mexico to aid in the Spanish Conquest in the sixteenth century.

The changes were great, from the large, highly bred, solid-colored Barbs to the small, sturdy, spotted mustangs, and yet one quality, more important than size or color, binds them together. It is the quality of adaptability, coupled with an unconquerable will to live. And it is this quality that the small but rugged Mexican mustang called Dragon had in great quantity.

Born in the Mexican mountains over twenty years ago, Dragon was captured at about the age of twelve, brought to Texas, and registered with the Pony of the Americas Club as Dragon No. 103. For three years he lived on a ranch near Dallas and sired the scores of outstanding POA ponies who were to bring him fame. These offspring bore not only Dragon's appaloosa markings but also his courage, stamina, intelligence, and spirit. Through them, Dragon became recognized as one of the foundation sires of the POA breed.

At around fifteen, an age when most horses are considered old, the little white freckled stallion began a new career that called for all the swiftness and sharpness of instinct that kept him alive in the wild. Under the loving hand of a young Iowa boy, he was broken to ride and learned the demanding art of Western performance competition. He was named an International Performance Champion in 1961 at the Third Annual International Pony of the Americas Show.

About the Author

Lynn Hall was born in a suburb of Chicago and was raised in Des Moines, Iowa. She has always loved dogs and horses and has kept them around her whenever possible. As a child, she was limited to stray dogs, neighbors' horses, and the animals found in library books. But as an adult, she has owned and shown several horses and has worked widely with dogs, both as a veterinarian's assistant and a handler on the dog show circuit. In recent years she has realized her lifelong dream of owning her own kennel and raising her own line of champion dogs; at her Touchwood Kennel she raises Bedlington terriers, which she shows throughout the country.

For several years Ms. Hall has devoted herself full-time to writing books for young readers, most of them about dogs and horses. Her book *A Horse Called Dragon* won the 1972 Charles W. Follett Award as a "worthy contribution to children's literature." *New Day for Dragon* is her fifteenth book to be published by Follett.

Ms. Hall lives in the village of Masonville, Iowa. Her leisure time is spent reading, playing the piano, or exploring the nearby hills and woodlands on horseback or foot, with a dog or two at her heels.

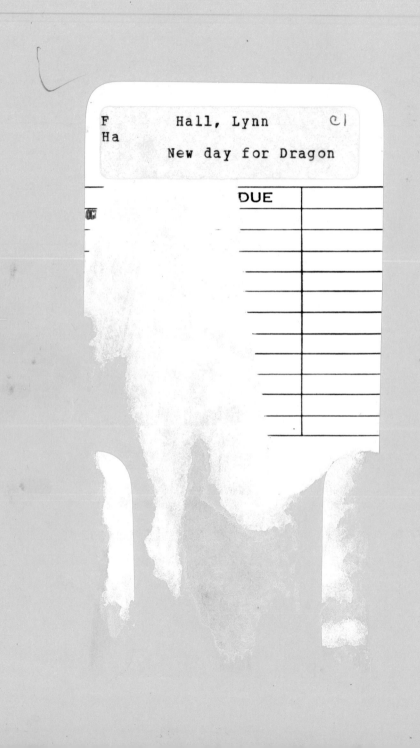